Cruz Control

Midnight Publications

La Redeaux

Cruz Control
La Redeaux

Cruz Control

ISBN-13: 978-0989119528
ISBN-10: 0989119521

www.laredeaux.com
Email: info@laredeaux.com

Give feedback on the book at:
contact@laredeaux.com

Printed in U.S.A

ACKNOWLEDGEMENTS

☙FOR THE READERS WHO GIVE NEW AUTHORS A CHANCE…THANK YOU!❧

IT'S YOU WHO INSPIRES ME!♣

Thank you to my editors E. Ruler and C. Curry

Special thanks to: Trae "Redbone" Ferguson, Carmen Blalock, Jeanette Sapphire Blue, Deidra Ds Green, Shantelle Brown, Anjela Day, Rhonda Amerson, Torrence Williams, Felecia Kelly, SiSTar Tea, Locksie Locks, Shai D and the entire ARC Book Club Inc., J'son M. Lee, Kim Morrow, Lisa Borders(Literary Divas), Tia Calloway, Papaya (Sistahs on Lit), Kendra MrsHoneyDip Littleton, Valerie Quinn, LaTonya Garrett, Rene Nightingale and Untamed.

To the numerous Facebook Bookclubs that allow me to mingle and promote. Far too many to mention. I never want to forget to thank someone, (*INSERT YOUR NAME HERE*) Thank you!

☙Enter the *RED ZONE*! ❧

La Redeaux

A vicious rumble of thunder erupted in the distance, followed by shards of lightening over the horizon. The rain fell in big hearty drops, pounding on the windshield of Shawnee's Freightliner Classic. Maneuvering her way through the intersection, she turned into the Flying J's truck stop. The location was packed already and it was barely eight o'clock. Finding a parking spot for the night would be nearly impossible. Pulling into the fuel island, she decided to face the interstate instead of fighting with the masses to park. Stepping out of her truck, she began to slip on the water and diesel soaked concrete. Hitting the cold, wet concrete would cause her to have to change her clothes and plans, she mused. Trying to balance herself against the fall, she was surprised by the hands gripping her waist. Being lifted in the air stunned her. Looking over her shoulder, she saw a familiar face smiling down at her.

"Still tripping over air I see," said Cruz in a deep throated rumble. Standing up straight she gazed at the 6'2" frame of the most insatiable man she'd ever seen. Smoothing out her clothes, she brushed her hair back into place before she responded.

"It's been a long time Cruz, are you still following me?" Shawnee asked.

"Only if you want me to," he replied.

Turning on her heel, she walked away from Cruz, heading inside the truck stop. She felt a sudden rush to get away from the man who called out to her innermost desires. Cruz was her ideal man. His tall frame, smooth cocoa butter skin and deep voice with a New York accent, sent shivers down her spine. Flashes of what almost happened six years ago danced in her eyes. His lips were hot and tender as he kissed her earlobes, teasing and whispering all at the same time. She could still taste his tongue on her mouth as she entered the station. Stopping at the counter,

Shawnee inquired how long the wait for showers would be. She would definitely need one now. Just thinking about him made her juices flow. The resistance she tried to build up came slowly tumbling down each and every time she saw him. While she waited on the attendants reply, he walked up behind her. Standing deathly close, she could feel his rock hard abs crushing against her back.

"Why do you make me chase you?" he asked.

"You don't have to chase me Cruz. I am positive that your dance card is longer than the Giants football field," she replied with a smirk.

"Hmm, that may be true, but I want you Shawnee. Yo, what do I have to do to prove that to you?"

Standing still, she tried to fight the sensations tingling through her body that threatened to explode, with every word he uttered. To avoid him from becoming her downfall, she had every intention of keeping up her resistance.

That man would have a woman looking for him in the daytime with a flashlight," she mused. Taking a deep breath, Shawnee's nostrils inhaled the aroma of his signature Issey Miyake cologne. Moving slightly out of his range, she turned around to look up in Cruz's dark eyes. She could see the embers of fire, dancing on his pupils while his smile glistened. She could feel the perspiration coating her forehead as words disappeared from her mind. Focusing on his tongue, she became engrossed in how it would really feel inside her honey pot. Shaking her head to remove the images, she finally found the strength to turn away from the vision of lust that captured her.

"You have nothing to prove to me Cruz. I know your type. You are a conqueror, and I won't be another notch in your belt."

"You're wrong, my Shawnee. I don't want to conquer you. I only want to fulfill your every desire. Imma show you how a *Real man* loves a woman," he stated.

His husky voice tormented her mind as the visions

took over. *She could feel his huge erection. His tongue played with her navel, stroking it in broad circles that led him down to the sweet muskiness of her private treasures. She moaned aloud.* The sound of her own voice brought her back to the reality. She was standing inside the truck stop waiting in line for a shower.

Turning back to face the attendant, she quickly grabbed her shower key and brushed right past him. She needed to get away from the essences of him, like the breath she needed to breathe. Walking briskly towards the back, she could her him calling out to her. She glanced back over her shoulder and saw him directly behind her. Stopping in her tracks she turned to him with her hands on her hips.

"What do you want Cruz?" she asked.

"You."

Before she could respond he backed her against the wall. Leaning in, he slipped his hands around her waist and buried his face in the softness of her neck. His tongue ran loops around her throbbing vein. Leaving a trail of heat in its wake, Cruz descended upon her mouth with a vengeance. His intention to make her want him as much as he needed her was obvious. She savored the flavor of his tongue, inhaling his essences until reality slapped her in the face. She tried to push Cruz's huge frame away from her. Breaking the dance, she scooted under his arm and raced into the shower. Closing the door behind her, she gripped her heart, hoping the pounding would cease and she could breathe normally again. She longed to release the pulsing between her thighs. However he would not get the satisfaction of knowing just how much she wanted him. She was determined not to be another one of his groupies. He had more than he could possibly handle. Stepping away from the door, she turned on the shower and stepped in fully clothed. She needed to soak herself before stripping. The cold blast could surely wash away the scent and taste that inflicted her at that very moment.

Cruz stood in the same place Shawnee had left him. *She was a slippery little minx,* he thought. Wiping his hand across his goatee, he smiled at the vision of her running to the shower room. He knew the effect he had on her. He just wondered why she was so tough and wouldn't give in. For six years he chased her on and off. He had let his one motto, '*Don't chase 'em, replace 'em!*' slip when it came to Shawnee. He wanted her that bad. Of course he had a slew of women throwing themselves at him on a regular basis, but Shawnee wasn't like the rest. She was the first woman he'd met that turned him down on the spot, without a second thought. She was blatant in her refusal to sleep with him on a casual basis or even go past first base.

The closest he'd ever gotten to tearing down her walls came after one night at *The Sports Bar*. Figuring he had too much to drink, she skidded out on him again. Remembering that night made him smile and shake his head. His boys clowned him for months after that scenario. He knew he needed to step up his game in order to deal with Shawnee. Her resistance heightened his curiosity, but that would be a matter to handle another time.

Deciding it was time to move, he headed towards the counter. He grabbed a Monster energy drink from the cooler. Not paying attention, he bumped into the attendant.

"Excuse me, sir," she said apologetically.

"Oh no my bad, I wasn't paying attention…Gina," Cruz stated pulling her name off her shirt.

"I've seen you in here several times. Who are you driving for?" Gina inquired.

"Strictly Business, my own company; I'm an owner operator."

"Hmm interesting how's business?"

"How you want my business?" Cruz asked, flirtatiously.

"On a table, inside and out," she seductively replied.

Feeling his manhood grow, Cruz eyed the slender attendant. He glanced back over his shoulder to see if Shawnee had perhaps emerged from the shower. Not seeing her in his main sight, Cruz eyed the attendant. She was shapely; however she could do something different with her hair. The ghetto styles some of the women preferred today did nothing for him. He preferred singular colored hair instead of the three or four colors she sported. She was way too dark to have green eyes Cruz thought. Gina stepped closer to Cruz inhaling his scent. She tossed her weave to the side and pressed her breast closer to him. She was forward. The type of woman he hit often and then lost their numbers. Having more time to kill before heading back to College Park, Cruz decided to give her what she wanted.

"What time is your break, Gina?" he asked.

"I'm on break now. Where's your girlfriend?" she questioned.

"Now why are you worried about things that don't concern you?"

"I'm just saying," Gina stated. "A man fine as you wouldn't be outta my sight, long If I were your girlfriend."

"No need to worry 'bout that," Cruz replied. "I'm single. So are you looking for Mr. Right or Mr. Right Now?"

"I've been waiting on Mr. Right for years, but you can be my Mr. Right Now," Gina stated.

"In that case Ms. Gina, let me pay for my items and I will meet you at the entrance in five minutes."

"No need, I'll take care of your items. Anything else you need?" Gina asked.

"Cool, nope that's everything."

Cruz handed Gina, his purchases and headed

towards the entrance. He left his truck in the fuel island. It was clearly marked Strictly Business. He was sure she had seen the fire red Freightliner classic before. He wasn't surprised she was so brazen in her approach. He had spotted her eyeing him while he talked with Shawnee. He knew an easy lay when he saw one. And since Shawnee still denied him, little" Miss Hot Pants" would do for now. Stepping up inside the luxury liner, Cruz pulled out his supply of sexual toys. He wondered what little Ms. Gina was into. Stroking his manhood, he checked his watch to see just how much time he had remaining. He watched the entrance to the Flying J, to see how long it would take her to emerge.

Right on cue, she walked out with an obscenely large purse slung over her shoulder. Cruz flashed his lights at her, indicating where he was. She strolled right on up to the truck and hopped up on the step. Cruz watched her mouth as she licked her lips and decided he wouldn't fuck Ms. Gina tonight, some good head would suffice. Gina wore her freak emblem like a badge of honor, so getting some head from her would be easy. Cruz pulled out the tropical flavored condoms and tossed them on his bunk. He would let her choose her own flavor. Let the freak swing wild tonight! He looked at her smiling widely at him and knew her gag reflex was good. Opening the door, Cruz slid out of the driver's seat to let Gina enter his domain. Just a tad bit of foreplay and he would have his dick in her mouth in no time. Gina entered the truck and dropped her satchel- like purse on the floor next to the gear shift. Looking around she admired the clean and tidy space. Her eyes landed on the bunk and the Durex flavored condoms Cruz threw on there just moments before. She glanced back up at him, delight dancing wildly in her eyes. Standing up she made her way into the cabin so effortlessly, Cruz wondered just how many times she had done this before.

"I see you are always prepared," Gina stated while picking up one of the banana flavored condoms.

"You never know what you'll need when traveling so I stay ready!" Cruz stated. "What do you have in your sack, Ms. Gina? That bag looks heavy."

"Nothing that applies to this, it's my homework, but I do have some Magnums inside. Like you, I don't have to get ready, I stay ready."

Taking his hands in hers, Gina placed the palms on her erect nipples. The games would begin immediately. She pulled him closer to her, sliding her hands down inside his pants. She felt his throbbing muscle grow larger. A sly smirk creased her mouth and her tongue emerged again. Cruz delighted in seeing that. He was ready to thrust all nine and a half inches down her throat. Taking out a towel from the cubby hole, Cruz prepared himself in case she could not handle all his girth. Releasing her breast, Cruz stepped back slightly out of her reach and slipped out of his jeans. Dropping the material to the floor, his manhood bounced as his hardness beckoned for attention. Gina gasped in awe of the vision before her eyes. She began to feel her juices flowing as she hurriedly pulled her own pants down to her ankles. Cruz reached over as she attempted to remove her shoes and halted her progress.

"That's not necessary," he stated. "The only thing you need to do is remove that gum and choose which condom to slip in your mouth. I don't plan to fuck you tonight. Just let you sample this goodness. Can you make me cum?"

Finally stepping out of the shower, Shawnee was still aroused with visions of Cruz. What made this man, drive her insane? Her resistance with men and their bull was strong. Until it came to Cruz! His strong jaw, neatly trimmed goatee, and dark chocolate eyes made him a delectable sight to any woman. But it was more than that for Shawnee. Yet she couldn't quite put her finger on the attraction. He sent a shiver of pure unadulterated desire down her spine. The awareness he elicited from her filled her entire body. It was a feeling she was unable to shake even after all these years. The celibate lifestyle she had practiced for the last three years threatened to give way every time she saw Cruz. He would definitely be her undoing. Keeping far away from the man was priority number one.

Stepping out of the shower room, Shawnee scanned

the drivers lounge to see if Cruz was laying in wake. Seeing the nearly deserted area, Shawnee through her bag over her shoulder and headed back to her truck. Stopping at the cooler, Shawnee bumped into the attendant who gave her the shower key.

"Oh, excuse me Miss," Shawnee stated.

"Sorry, my fault!" Gina replied. "I'm late coming from my break I wasn't paying attention."

"Well tell them you were helping out in the laundry area. No need to get in trouble for a few extra minutes," Shawnee stated handing Gina her book.

"Thanks!" "Do you drive alone or with someone? You don't look like the typical female driver. Most of them that come in here are so mannish looking it's scary," Gina stated.

Chuckling to herself, Shawnee replied, "No I drive alone and thanks for the compliment."

Turning and grabbing a Coke out the cooler, the

faint woodsy and citrus spice wafted up Shawnee's nose.
Stopping dead in her tracks, Shawnee inhaled deeply. She
knew that fragrance anywhere. Glancing around the aisle,
the only other person in the aisle was Gina the attendant.
Taking a few subtle steps backwards, Shawnee inhaled
again to make sure she wasn't confused. The aroma grew
stronger. Turning on her heels, Shawnee strolled back in
the direction of Gina and inhaled once more. Shaking her
head, Shawnee eyed the attendant. Unable to formulate
a proper chain of thought, Shawnee stood there with her
mouth agape.

"Did you forget something?" Gina asked.

"No, um that's an interesting fragrance you have
on. What's it called?"

Standing with her mouth open, Gina bowed her
head and sniffed at her shirt. Before she could respond,
Shawnee walked away, leaving her standing there. Her
blood began to boil. She was furious. *Then again,* she
thought to herself. *Why get mad. He's not your man,*

Shawnee. Standing at the counter, Shawnee's cell phone rang a familiar tune. She needed not look down to see whom it was, Aaliyah's One in a Million was set to only one person. Cruz. Undoubtedly he'd sent her a text message or voicemail. Shawnee reached down to silence the phone, when she felt a tap on her shoulder.

"Miss," Gina began. "Can I talk to you for a second?"

Inhaling his strong scent again, Shawnee looked the attendant up and down before she spoke. The one-sided look on her face must have been evident as the attendant lowered her head, grabbing Shawnee's hand and stepping away from the counter.

"I know what you're thinking," Gina began. "But nothing happened."

"Really," Shawnee stated. "Is that why you smell like him?"

"I was believe me, I was! Just as we were about

to begin, He got a text message. He stopped me COLD! He mumbled something about stepping up his game, and eliminating people. Then we sat there and talked about me and school," Gina confessed.

"WOW! I don't know if I should believe you or not but a word of advice, don't drop your drawers for every man that lights your fire."

"Well he's obviously into you. Your picture popped up on his screensaver. Why aren't you interested?"

"It's simple, everything that glitters ain't gold."

At that statement, Shawnee turned around and headed out of the truck stop. She had already wasted way too much of her time in there as it was. She needed to get in a nap before heading down to Miami the next day. Thoughts of Cruz were the last thing she needed to be focused on. He was trouble walking. No sooner than the thought passed through her mind, her cell rang again. This time it was Beyoncé's Crazy in Love 'I just don't understand how your love can do what no one else can.'

Shawnee woke with a start, finding that she was drenched in sweat or better yet in heat, since what had awakened her was another erotic dream.

Cruz had touched her, kissed her, made love to her. Her moans of protest soon became moans of pleasure. At the exact moment when he was about to finish off the mind-blowing foreplay and enter her royal orifice, declaring himself king, she awakened.

Shawnee pulled herself up into the sitting position trying to calm the raging inferno burning between her thighs. Wetness covered her body like a veil, just another sign that she was still in denial about her feelings for Cruz. For a brief moment it all felt so real. The way his bald head felt beneath her palm as he nibbled on her breast while his fingers weaved through her hair. She could feel the weight of his solid muscles pressed against her body. She was so caught up in the sheer feel of him, that every nerve in her body was set ablaze.

Throwing the covers off with disgust, Shawnee set

up in her bunk. After three years of celibate life and six years of knowing Cruz, he still lit a fire inside no other man has. It perplexed her something wicked. She was able to withstand the advances of men easily but Cruz she could not seem to shake. Stretching out she glanced down at her soaked boy shorts and then at the bed. Her body had betrayed her once again. Just the thoughts of him inside her gave way to orgasmic rushes she couldn't control. Stripping her clothes off, she cursed her body for betraying her once again.

Since sleep would elude her any further tonight Shawnee, jumped in the driver's seat. Turning the key, her freight shaker roared to life. *Get some miles under your belt,* she thought to herself. Pressing the clutch, Shawnee shifted her truck into gear and pulled out of the truck stop. She reached over and turned the radio on to 93.3 just in time to hear Young Jeezy's beat blast out the speakers, Leave You Alone. *Perfect,* Shawnee mused, *just what I need.* A man telling me why I need to leave that alone. Singing along with the song and changing the words around, Shawnee played the melody loudly.

"You ain't no good, but you feel so good. I would if I could but I got to leave you alone. You bad and I want you bad, but I won't give you the satisfaction…I'm leaving you alone."

Just as she was getting out of the hook, her cell rang. Screaming at the top of her lungs, she turned the radio down and pressed answer on her Bluetooth.

"Talk to me!"

"Damn, girl is that how you answer the phone these days?" Linda asked.

"Um yeah, I knew it was you."

"Where are you at tonight?"

"Headed to Miami, you working tonight?"

"Ooh you gonna see Ricky Rozay in South Beach tonight!" Linda laughed.

"Ugh, now I know you know good and damn well

I ain't hitting South Beach in this big ass truck."

"Well anyways, I was just calling to check on you."

"Thanks but you cut my song off, I was just about to run the lyrics down. You not gonna believe who I ran into AGAIN!"

"Oh man, who did you run into 'cause girl I swear you got the worse luck with men."

"CRUZ."

"I take that back then. I hope you gave up the cookies, 'cause your eggs 'bout to dry the fuck up."

"HELL NO! I told you I am not hooking up with that man. I want to keep the mind I have and fucking 'round with Cruz would have me Looney Tunes."

"Shit I don't know how you do it! I would be dropping it like it's hot."

"And that's exactly what he expects. Every woman swooning over his ass. The damn clerk at the truck stop was about to drop it for him."

"NOOOOOOO!"

"Girl yeah, you know I can smell his ass a mile away. She was smelling like him but says they didn't make that far 'cause I texted his ass and they stopped."

"You texted him? What you said?"

"NEVER KISS ME AGAIN, UNLESS I ASK, I DON'T NEED A PLAYA I NEED A REAL MAN!"

"Wow, what did he say?"

"You know his smug ass got smart with me talking about you know you love my lips, just as much as you love me. Stop fighting the fire."

"Humph, well he wasn't lying?" Linda snickered.

"Girl bye, you ain't supposed to agree with the enemy!"

Hanging up the phone, Shawnee's laughter continued to fuel her drive. She knew she should've stayed parked but, putting miles behind her was the best option. Cruz brought out intense feelings she was not ready to face. Yet every time she saw him, she was reminded why she needed to keep the walls up.

Lowering the window down, Shawnee flipped her favorite playlist on, and set the cruise control. She still had a six hour drive time before she would arrive down in Miami. As the music caressed her ears, she hoped she would have a quick turn around and head back to Atlanta for the weekend.

Just south of Atlanta, Cruz pulled into the Love's Truck stop. He was ready to get out of his rig. Being able to make his own deliveries was a blessing and a curse, sometimes. However in his eyes money was money. And aside from women and bikes, that was something he couldn't get enough of. This weekend he would be attending his motorcycle club event. There would definitely be someone there that would take his mind off Shawnee, and showing off his latest custom built tricycle was an added bonus. This year he had lined up quite a few models to help showcase Strictly Business.

Stepping into his midnight black Ford Expedition, Cruz's thoughts drifted back to Shawnee. She wasn't like any of the other women he dated. She was fiercely independent and strong willed. She possessed qualities that reminded him of the resilient women in his own family. His mother stayed on his back constantly about finding a 'good woman', settling down and giving her some grandkids. Thoughts of his mother, reminded him of her text earlier. He'd invited Shawnee over to dinner with his family six years ago and his mother still asked every year if she was coming to another event. Shawnee had made quite an impression on her. Not only had she shown up dressed like he'd never seen her before, she came bearing gifts.

The rare Swarovski Crystal Maxi Dolphin still sat on the mantel. Every time she had guests, that damn dolphin made an appearance. His father was no better, he mused. Shawnee had given him a Refraction Crystal Limited Edition Chess Set, that she'd found at a yard sale for fifty dollars. He was so impressed he did a Google search on the chess set. After the initial shock had worn off, he tried unsuccessfully to give the set back to Shawnee. Shawnee had driven up for a private dinner and listened to Derrick Sr. explain why she needed to take the expensive set back. She had no idea that the chess set was worth more than eight grand when she gave it to him, and she simply refused to take it back. Cruz could still hear his Father raving about the set at Christmas. His parents were so impressed with Shawnee they hated every other woman he dated. He'd finally broken things down to them after Sunday dinner one afternoon. He and Shawnee were friends; he explained that she had made it clear to him that she wasn't interested in a relationship with him.

His mother wouldn't hear it. She told him, "Of course not, what woman wants a boy pretending to be a man? Grow up son," she'd hissed. He'd never disrespected his mother, so he just listened to her. Pulling into his assigned spot at his condo, Cruz stroked his goatee. He decided to invite Shawnee over for Thanksgiving dinner. He hoped she didn't have plans. His sister would be home this year and it would be the perfect time for her to meet. Maybe she could help his dilemma 'cause he was currently batting zero.

During the next couple of days, Cruz busied himself preparing for the weekend at the Peachtree 8th Annual Bike Fest. He hadn't thought about Shawnee until his mother called to say she was in Atlanta for the weekend. Completely thrown off with that bit of information, Cruz thought about texting Shawnee. He was sure she said she would be in Miami. At any rate he definitely would have to modify his plans if she was in town. He would call his mother back shortly to find out all the information. If Shawnee was coming to Atlanta this weekend, he would need to make some preparations. He was intent on pulling out all the stops. He knew that dropping the playboy bravado would be essential if he wanted her to take him seriously. Shawnee would see him in a different light after this weekend.

Everything was falling into place and the execution was flawless at Bike Fest. The only thing that would make the day any better in Cruz's eyes would be seeing Shawnee. She had arrived at his mother's house just like she said. He wasn't able to make an appearance there as of yet. It wouldn't have mattered anyway since his sister Hollyn and his mother had taken Shawnee to the mall. The threesome was having a girl's day out. He made Hollyn promise to come by the event. He hadn't seen them yet so he figured they were still out shopping. Cruz did all that he could do to keep the woman out of his mind.

Meanwhile on the other side of town, the topic of constant discussion was Cruz and Shawnee. Hollyn quizzed Shawnee relentlessly over everything about herself. If it weren't for Mrs. Black, Shawnee wouldn't have gotten a chance to think of anything else. Interrupting her chain of thought Shawnee responded to each and every question with the honest truth. Before they left the mall Shawnee's request to go by Cruz's bike event left both of the women excited and shocked at the same time. Mrs. Black finally heard exactly what she needed to hear.

"My dear," she began, "Derrick is just like his father. Before we married thirty years ago, he had a slew of women at his beck and call. I must admit you and I are more alike than you realize. I never had any interest in his player ways. He pursued me. When I finally agreed to court him, he did a three sixty on me. The women were a thing of the past and the sex, excuse me but I think you youngsters today call it 'The BOMB'. You can save the protest and denial, Sweet Pea. I can see it in your eyes every time someone mentions Cruz. The flame that burns in your eyes, I know all too well, so do yourself and me a favor. Get that boy to settle down and give me some more grandkids.

Shawnee sat there listening to Mrs. Black talk on

and on about Cruz and wondered if she was right. *Could Cruz turn in his Playa card for life? Would she be able to trust a man that had women swoon over him all the time? Could she really make a life with him?* Before she could finish her tirade of thoughts assaulting her mind, her cell phone rang. Answering the call, Shawnee excused herself from the table.

"Talk to me."

"Girl did you make it to Atlanta yet?" Linda asked.

"Yeah, I got here last night I am at the mall with Mrs. Black and Hollyn."

"Who is Hollyn?"

"Cruz's sister, she's hilarious and a trip."

"Does he know you are there yet?"

"I am pretty sure he does by know. I checked into the DoubleTree near the airport before going over to his mom's house for dinner last night. They asked me to go shopping today and dinner tomorrow. We are getting ready to stop by the bike fest after we leave here."

"Okay well I am not going to keep you long, but are you gonna clear those cob webs out tonight? Don't be scared forever, give up the cookies."

"Dammit girl bye." Shawnee laughed out loud before hanging up on her long time friend.

Walking back to the table, Shawnee placed her phone down just as another text message crossed the screen. Before she could answer it, Hollyn grabbed her phone and jumped up from the table singing and dancing, "I'm gonna finally get a sister, sister, sister, won't you be my sister." Shawnee and Mrs. Black erupted in laughter at Hollyn. Although she was dead serious the look on her face was comical. Hollyn placed her hands on her hips and poked out her lips. "Fine," she said, "I will just have to answer my brother with a message that will knock his socks off for you. You are too slow. And I think you need a serious boost in the romantic area," Hollyn squealed. Shawnee stood up trying to get her phone from Hollyn before she sent a message that Shawnee would have to explain. Mrs. Black sat back looking at the girls tousle as tears of laughter built up in her eyes. She was sure that Shawnee would make a great daughter-in-law and Hollyn liked her, which was surprising. Hollyn never liked any of her brothers, girlfriends. And now here she was playing with Shawnee like they hadn't just met last night. Mrs. Black was filled with joy at the sight. Interrupting them Mrs. Black stated, "If we want to catch the last of the event you girls better finish up this cheesecake so we can go." Hollyn stopped at her mother's voice and looked at her slice of cake. Tossing Shawnee her phone, Hollyn picked up her tray and tossed the contents in the trash receptacle. "Done. Let's go because I have to see this meeting with my own eyes." Shawnee couldn't get a word in before Hollyn began talking about her brother again. She was like a walking, talking advertisement. If it weren't for Mrs. Black's interruptions, the entire conversation to the stadium would have been about Cruz.

Shawnee was glad for the musical interlude; she now had the time to get her thoughts together. She replayed her conversation with Linda over in her mind. She wasn't afraid of Cruz. The only thing that scared her was the thought of getting her heartbroken again. A slight giggle escaped her at the thought of coochie cobwebs. Linda always had a way of putting things that made her laugh. Shawnee knew it had been quite a long time since she'd been with a man. Cruz would more than likely break her hymen in to pieces. Shawnee began to feel her moistness as she sat and thought about Cruz. She decided at that moment tonight would be the night. Whether they became a couple or not, Shawnee was going to sample the waters. And if she had any luck, she would dive in more than once.

An hour later they arrived at the stadium. Shawnee was a nervous wreck. *What if Cruz had other plans?* She knew his dance card was always full. So she wondered if he would even have the time to see her at all. As they made their way over to Strictly Business' booth, that question was put to rest. Cruz walked up to them, scooping up Shawnee effortlessly and placing a kiss on her forehead before hugging and acknowledging his mother and sister.

"Is that the way you greet your sister and mother,"

Hollyn asked. "As a second thought?"

"Shut up Lil girl," Cruz replied.

"Whatever, Niiii…" Hollyn began.

"Y'all haven't scared off my future wife have you?" Cruz asked.

Stunned into silence the three women turned around with open mouths to look in the direction of the words. Mrs. Black spoke up first, "I have to leave, your daddy is texting me. Momma's got a date." Hollyn distorted her face, before she screamed, "Ugh…Mom TMI, TMI, TMI!!!" Laughter erupted in unison as Mrs. Black grabbed Hollyn's hand leading her away. "Cruz, take care of Shawnee." She laughed. Dragging Hollyn by the hand, Mrs. Black waved bye to Cruz and Shawnee who stood there with her mouth open. She was in shock. Mrs. Black had just set her up. She shook her head slightly mused. Cruz gazed down at Shawnee who watched the duo retreat towards the parking area. Shawnee heaved a deep breath before looking at Cruz. She knew he was

42

staring at her, she could feel his eyes burning paths across her body. Finally breaking the silence, Cruz stated, "Penny for your thoughts?" Using the old school song, Shawnee replied, "Nickel for your kiss. And a Dime if you tell me you love me."

Clasping her hands to her mouth quickly, the words had already escaped before she could think. Leaning in Cruz placed his mouth centimeters away from Shawnee's and whispered ever so sweetly, "Keep your nickel and that was a question so I can kiss you now." And he did. Cruz devoured Shawnee's mouth with passion. They were standing directly in front of his booth. While the models and everyone watched, Cruz kissed Shawnee with a passion he'd never displayed before. Their kiss was broken by the applause that flared up in the background. He hadn't seen his boys walk over or even heard the models whisper. He was caught up in the worst kind of way. Shawnee's face was flush by the time their lips parted ways. She stood there wrapped in Cruz's arms looking at the crowd that had emerged. You would've thought they were celebrities or something. Shawnee's face turned three shades of red. She felt like a love struck teen, Cruz had her blood flowing in the most intimate of places. She could no longer resist the man. Tonight she would give in to temptation of lust and pray that her heart could withstand.

∽∾∽∾∽∾∽∾∽∾∽∾∽

Four hours later, Shawnee was standing at the door of Cruz's condo. A tantalizing sensation snaked down her spine in anticipation of what was to come. She turned to walk away and stopped, as the words of her friend rang inside her head. Turning back around, Shawnee knocked lightly on the door. Remembering the passionate kiss from earlier, Shawnee knocked harder this time landing three full pounds on the door.

Moments later, Cruz was standing in the doorway, stark naked dripping wet. Her eyes roved over his tall frame watching the drops of water drizzle down his chest, abdomen, to his semi flaccid dick. Shawnee gasped audibly before looking in Cruz's eyes.   She wanted to speak but the words would not escape her mouth as they both stood there staring at each other in the doorway. Stepping to the side Cruz reached out and took Shawnee's hand and ushered her into his home.

He continued to look at her long and hard, making her already heated body much hotter. She was fully aroused and he knew it. She thought she could no longer stand the intensity of his heated gaze, when he smiled and that sexy curve enhanced his masculine features. Her body reacted in the most primitive ways; exploding desire wafted through every inch of her being. Just when she thought she could no longer maintain the slightest composure, Cruz closed the distance between them. Shawnee's heart began to pound in her chest. A nervous quiver ran down her spine.

"Are you sure you're ready for this?" Cruz whispered, taking her hand and pulling her closer to his naked frame. The closeness allowed her to feel his erection as it grew. Shawnee closed her eyes, and willed her screaming mind that bellowed a resounding no over and over to quiet and answered with her pulsing body.

"I've never been sure about anything with you Cruz. But tonight I am sure that I want you," Shawnee whispered.

That was all the answer Cruz needed, he scooped her into his arms and carried her into his bedroom. Placing her on the bed gently, Cruz removed her heels and slid his hand upwards: a devilish smile crossed his face when he realized Shawnee had come to him with nothing on. Standing erect over her he saw the shyness cross her face turning her cheeks red with yearning. Cruz ripped open the light trench coat she wore sending buttons flying in every direction. Revealing her nakedness for him to see, before she could utter a word, Cruz took her nipple into his warm mouth. Cruz licked and sucked the first one before descending on the other. With each tug sensuous sensations rippled through her body. His mouth played ping pong with her breast as his hands explored and caressed parts of her body. Releasing her breast, Cruz placed kisses along her body.

"Do you trust me, Shawnee?" Cruz asked between kisses.

"I am here. I trust you now," she said breathlessly.

"I want to take you to Loveland. I want us to go together to experience the kind of pleasure that only the two of us can generate." His voice dropped an octave, when he asked, "Will you go with me?"

Shawnee swallowed when his knuckles grazed her thighs and his hands stroked her bare mound. Cruz continued to stroke her. "I want to take you on one hell of an adventure. Are you ready?"

Biting back a moan, she opened her eyes locking them with Cruz. She replied, "Yes!"

Closing her eyes she knew her face betrayed her as the flush of sensation overhauled her senses. She melted inside with the thoughts of what he was about to do to her. Her heart was pounding erratically in her chest as the feathery touch of his fingers slowly drove her insane. Cruz prepared to send her over the edge when he replaced his fingers with his mouth.

Shawnee's body bucked wildly at the first touch of his tongue. A deep groan escaped her throat when he proceeded to taste her with a hunger that appeared unquenched. She clutched the bedspread in need of something to hold on to. His mouth was driving her insane. Shawnee clenched her lip between her teeth in an effort to stop herself from screaming. Cruz retracted his mouth long enough to say, "Let go baby, come for me."

No sooner than he replaced his mouth on her, Shawnee came. The force of the climax hit her harder than a Mack truck. Her senses gathered in one location making her forget everything. It was impossible for her to hold back. Shawnee screamed out his name as her body split into thousands of tiny pieces. Waves of pleasure washed over her. She cried out several more times while Cruz transported her body, mind and soul to the place where desire resided. Loveland.

Cruz pulled back and watched the wave of emotions

of Shawnee's orgasms move through her body. For six years he dreamed of this moment. The only thing he wanted to do was sit there and inhale her womanly scent and savor her taste in his mouth. Hearing Shawnee scream out his name over and over filled him with joy that he'd never felt before. He knew that he was in store for a ride that would give him passions like no other had.

With the intense need to control the remainder of her body and mind, Cruz reached into the side drawer and pulled out a condom. He slipped it on quickly wanting and needing to feel the depths of her insides encase his manhood. He eased back to the center of the bed and joined Shawnee. Their faces were inches apart as their gazes met and their lips locked in the sweetest kiss Cruz had ever felt. Shawnee pulled back as a smile creased her mouth. "I came!" she said in amazement. Tracing his lips with the tip of his tongue, Cruz smiled back. "Yes you did, but it's not over yet, you might lose count."

Before she could protest, Cruz kissed her in a way that let her know it was getting ready to go down again.

He released her mouth, and began to rain kisses down her neck leaving a trail of passion in his wake. He devoured her breasts as he had done earlier and placed his fingers in the flesh he'd savored.

"Cruzzzzz," she called out his name.

"Open your eyes Shawnee," Cruz stated. He wanted to see her eyes the moment he joined flesh to flesh with her. Love and desire pulsed through his veins, making his erection harder and thicker. When she glanced in his eyes, she knew he needed her just as much as she needed him. Taking his hand he raised her hands above her head and interlocked his fingers within his. With his free hand, he slowly eased one finger inside her, then adding a second he found her tighter than he imagined. Her tightness excited him even more. "Cruz," came the breathless whisper from Shawnee, "take me, and take me now." His response was a hard thrust, which barely took in all of his erection. Pulling back Cruz thrust so hard it shook him to his core. Shawnee arched her body beneath him and matched his thrust. As Cruz moved in and out, her moans grew louder and more intense, commanding him to stroke harder and faster. Their rhythm matched the fierceness that grew in their eyes.

Cruz felt the explosion begin to rip through her body. Her fingers dug into his back and her legs locked around his waist and he kept making love to her. The reality was better than any woman Cruz ever had. He moved in and out intensifying both their pleasures with every motion, feeling the urgency building up in Shawnee, his own needs came forth.

The next eruption triggered his own and they screamed out each other's name at the same time. Taking her mouth one last time, Cruz locked everything he had in a deep kiss. The electricity sent waves coursing throughout both of their bodies. Minutes later after the waves subsided, Cruz was far too weak and too satisfied to release Shawnee from his arms. Turning to the side he managed to shift their bodies and lie on his back while maintaining the connection. Feeling the aftermath of what has just happened Shawnee buried her face into Cruz's neck and wrapped her legs and arms around him.   Exhausted and well spent they both drifted off into sheer bliss.

Shawnee awoke with the lingering effects of the night before. The hard body pressed against her back sent a smile across her face. She stretched a little and reached to caress the masculine arms the embraced her. Shawnee scooted closer into Cruz's embrace and felt a stiff hard-on pressing in her back. A devilish grin crossed Cruz lips and in one swift movement he maneuvered his body atop of Shawnee.

Shawnee moved quickly sliding down beneath Cruz, with puckered lips she placed three kisses on his rippled abs. She wrapped her palm around his rock hard shaft massaging it as she trailed kisses down his center. Landing her lips over the tip of his erection, Cruz moaned, "Damn." He made an upward thrust of his hips pushing himself deeper into her mouth. Her head job had him primed to a point where Cruz reached an intensifying level. With her tongue, lips and teeth Shawnee sucked and tugged and licked every inch of his shaft with the right precision. She applied the right amount of pressure stimulating him beyond imagination with every stroke. When she sent him to the brink of eruption, she pulled back and delivered a blowing stream of cool air over his flaming flesh. Taking the glass from the nightstand, Shawnee sipped some of the cool water before replacing her water filled mouth back over the tip of his penis. The coolness of the water brought Cruz to a thundering climax as he screamed loudly.

"Oh damn," Cruz bellowed over and over again. On the brink of release Cruz fought to reclaim his manhood from Shawnee's grasp. He refused to waste this seed, he wanted to feel her flesh as he released. Guiding her upwards, he smiled while using his knee to spread her legs further apart. In a singular motion Cruz entered Shawnee with fierceness. Wrapping her legs around his waist, she matched his thrust. Cruz moved steadily delivering slow easy strokes that helped him regain his composure. He placed one hand over her breast thumbing her nipples with circular motions. He played rhythmic numbers with his hand while delighting himself in the melodic moans coming from Shawnee.

Without withdrawing from Shawnee's velvet casing, Cruz flipped over on his back landing Shawnee above him. Glaring down in his eyes, Shawnee bounced and bucked wildly on top of Cruz. Turning positions she created a viselike grip as she rocked back and forth giving Cruz ample view of her rear. Cruz moved beneath her faster and his thrust became stronger as growls erupted from his core.

"Give it to me! Ride this dick baby! Ahhh!" Cruz roared. "It's all mine," Shawnee replied. "Give it to me!"

Unable to control the urge for release, Cruz sat up enfolding Shawnee in his arms. He fondled her breast as she rotated circular motions over his manhood. As Shawnee spiraled into her release she felt the throbbing pulsating of Cruz's beginning. With his body molded into hers their release came simultaneously. Shawnee could feel his heart beating through her back as their erotic morning subsided.

After emerging from the shower Shawnee found Cruz leaning over the kitchen counter. Walking up behind him, she smacked him hard on his rear. Looking up she shook her hand quickly trying to ease the sting. "Must you be hard everywhere?" she giggled while eyeing his naked chest.

"That's what you get, Shawnee!" Cruz laughed. "I am the only one that will be smacking asses around here. Now come here woman, let me look at that hand." Racing around the counter, Shawnee stuck her tongue out at Cruz before squealing out a resounding, "NOO!"

"I am going to catch you little lady. Did you forget you're in my house?" Cruz stated.

Taking two long strides, Cruz was face to face with Shawnee. Placing another kiss on her forehead, he raised her hand to his mouth and kissed it too. Shawnee playfully attempted to pull her hand back. Cruz wrapped his free hand around her waist before speaking pulling her closer into his embrace.

"You know I like a chase, Shawnee. We'll just have to save that for later though. Hollyn just called and said they were waiting on us to have brunch," Cruz said.

"We'll drive in together, let me throw on a shirt and grab a couple of things."

"My car is in the parking lot, I can drive myself," Shawnee replied.

"And if you do that I won't be able to caress those thighs, Shawnee. Would you do that to a brother? Deprive him of something so delectable? Huh?"

Laughing at the pitiful face Cruz had imposed on her, Shawnee gave Cruz her keys and overnight bag.

Twenty minutes later, seated in the driver's seat, Cruz glanced over at Shawnee and placed his hands as promised on her thighs, stroking them tenderly while pulling out the lot. Cruz felt her tense up as they entered the highway enroute to his family home.

"Is everything okay, babe?" Cruz asked.

"Yes, I'm fine just wondering what your parents are going to say when we pull up together."

"Relax babe, Cruz got everything under control."

Leaning back Shawnee tried to relax unsuccessfully. She was a bundle of nerves. She had a good relationship with his parents and even liked his sister. She just didn't want this to end badly. She wanted a family and deep down she knew Cruz would make the perfect father.

Cruz turned on his soothing playlist and the local saxophonist blared through the speakers doing renditions of some of the greatest love songs to ever cross the airwaves. Shawnee opened her eyes momentarily surprised that Cruz listened to jazz. Giving him a side-eyed glance she adjusted her seat belt and closed her eyes once again.

Pulling into the driveway of his parents' house thirty minutes later, Cruz jumped out of the truck and ran into the front yard when he saw Hollyn rolling on the grass with an unknown woman. The cries of a small child caught his attention. Pulling his sister up by the collar, Cruz finally recognized the woman Hollyn was assaulting.

"Jennifer? What the hell? Hollyn what's going on here?" Cruz shouted.

"Ask that bitch," Hollyn slurred.

Struggling out of his grasp, Jennifer walked backwards towards her open car door. Grabbing her purse out of her car, she cried and screamed uncontrollably. No one could make out what she was saying. Clearly intoxicated, her words were slurred and her eye was visibly swollen. Cruz turned to Hollyn with a puzzled look on his face. Hollyn began to scream again, while struggling to get unconstrained from her brothers grip. "Let me go Derrick," Hollyn screamed. "I ain't nowhere near finished teaching that bitch a lesson. How dare she come up here drunk and disrespect My Momma," Hollyn continued with her tirade until she noticed Shawnee walking towards her and Derrick. "Calm down," Cruz ordered Hollyn. She was still heated and intent on finishing her rumbles with Jennifer. Cruz looked at Shawnee and asked her to escort Hollyn in the house.

"I ain't going anywhere!" Hollyn screamed at Cruz. The venom in her voice was evident as she rolled her eyes at Cruz. Hollyn turned back to her old high school friend Jennifer and spit on the ground. She was finally able to loosen the grip Cruz had on her and began dancing back and forth. Cruz glanced down at her, before his eyes landed again on Jennifer. She looked a hot mess. Her tri-colored lace front wig was nearly ripped from her head. The short skirt she wore was dirty and her shirt was ripped, evidence she had tousled with Hollyn. Cruz hadn't seen Jennifer in more than eight years. She definitely looked nothing like she had before. The cries of the small child brought Cruz's attention to his parents standing on the porch. His mother was holding the hand of a boy who looked to be around four or five years old. Cruz turned back around to find Jennifer waving a gun in the air.

"Calm down Jennifer," Cruz began.

"Don't tell me to be calm, tell that bitch ass sister of yours."

"Jennifer, listen to me. It's Cruz. You know I don't do drama. Calm down and tell me what's wrong?"

"You know what's wrong, Deeerrrriick," Jennifer slurred.

"How 'bout this, let's go for a ride, Jennifer."

"I ain't going nowhere with yo ass!"

"Jennifer, what's wrong?"

"Everything's wrong Cruz! You broke your promise to me but you gonna keep your promise to Lil D."

"Jennifer, what are you talking about?"

Hollyn interrupted the conversation, screaming, "That drunk ho's claiming that boy is yours Derrick!" Turning around facing Hollyn, Cruz's distorted face spoke volumes. He knew he'd never slept with Jennifer and confusion was one thing he despised. Before he could respond, he heard Shawnee gasp. Looking in her direction, he saw anger building inside her eyes. Seeing the escalating doom, Mrs. Black ushered Shawnee inside the house. Cruz turned back towards Hollyn. "Is that why you are out here acting like a hood rat, Hollyn?" Cruz slurred.

Hollyn turned and landed a punch square in Cruz's stomach. "Hood rat, D?" Hollyn yelled. "I am not the hood rat. That bitch over there is. Everybody knows you can buy her ass for a dime!" Standing erect Cruz grabbed Hollyn, "Stop tormenting her Hollyn. I did promise to look after her if she called me," Cruz stated. Then turning to Jennifer, "You never called me Jenn. How do you expect me to help you if you never called me?" Cruz slowly started to walk towards Jennifer, in an attempt to calm her and get the gun from her hand. She didn't need to hurt herself or anyone else for that matter. As he approached her, Jennifer slouched to her knees. Cruz could smell the alcohol and mix of weed emitting from her body. She was slurring words that he couldn't make out.

Suddenly Jennifer jumped up as if something had sparked a fire within her. BAM BAM BAM! The shots rang out quickly as Hollyn and Cruz hit the ground. Raising his head up, Cruz crawled the distance to where Jennifer lay with blood pouring from her stomach. Cruz kicked the gun away from her open palm and yelled to Hollyn to call the ambulance. The shock of what just transpired had Hollyn frozen in place, tears streamed down her eyes as memories of her playing with her childhood friend Jennifer ran through her mind. Standing in the doorway, Shawnee had the emergency operator on the line. With the little boy, wrapped around her leg, Shawnee could feel his tears streaming as he cried out for his mother. Shawnee was still in awe of what had just taken place. She spoke with the 911 operator as calmly as she could, urging them to respond quickly. When she saw Cruz finally stand, his blood stained shirt, made Shawnee jump from the porch and run to him. Running her hands up and down his shirt, Shawnee clutched him close to her.

The sight of so much blood had her heart beating at a rapid pace. She could barely keep her heart inside her chest. She locked her arm around Hollyn whom had come and stood beside the both of them. The tears streaming down her face displayed the sadness that had replaced the anger she felt earlier. Shawnee was still slightly confused about the whole situation, but she was glad that her Cruz was still here with her. Shawnee felt Hollyn disengage herself from their group hug. Shawnee watched her walk back towards the porch and the little boy whom had latched himself onto her mother's leg now. He eased to the other side of Mrs. Black as Hollyn approached him. Mrs. Black took Hollyn in her arms; while rubbing her back soothingly telling her everything will be okay. Cruz turned his attention back to Shawnee. He knew it was time for him to make a life of his own. He was intent on keeping his promise to Lil D, something that he had let slip with Jenn.

Reaching inside his pocket, Cruz thumbed the little black box he planned to give to Shawnee over brunch. Heaving a deep sigh he knew today wouldn't be appropriate, at least if he wanted the correct answer. He would wait until the time was right. For now he knew he had some explaining to do as the sounds of the ambulance and police cars emerged on the street.

Pulling apart from Shawnee, Cruz placed a kiss on her forehead and ushered her inside. He took Hollyn's hand and pulled her from their mother's grasp. Cruz informed Hollyn she would have to speak to the officers and explain what happened before he arrived. He assured her that everything would be okay. Walking off the porch, Cruz glanced back at Shawnee as she leaned over and picked up the little boy. She placed her hand behind Mrs. Black and

ushered her and Lil D. inside the house.

Standing there Cruz spoke with the officers and explained his relationship to Jennifer. Five years ago, he had found her outside of his shop as he prepared to open for the day. Jennifer was laying there half naked and disoriented. Her face was bloody and swollen. He barely recognized her as his sister's childhood friend. When she called him by his given name, he knew immediately who she was. Cruz stated that he never opened the shop that day; instead he loaded Jennifer in his truck and drove her to Memorial Hospital. He stayed with her the entire two days. Jennifer had been out at a bar the night prior and was gang raped and beaten. That day, he promised to help her in any way that he could. She was a promiscuous girl as a teen and after both her parents were killed during her first year in college, Jennifer had taken a downward spiral. She dropped out of college and was a regular in the local low life bars. It had been rumored that she was a regular coke head, selling her body for a hit. She however had sworn to Cruz that wasn't the case. She was a broken-hearted girl and Cruz saw that. He felt guilty that he hadn't reached out to do more to help her before now. After her son was born, she named him Derrick. She asked Cruz to be his godfather. He'd given her money on a couple of occasions to buy the boy things he needed. Cruz explained that he hadn't seen Jennifer in the past two years. He told the officers, he'd went to her last address he had and she no longer lived there. He assumed she had moved with some relatives she had in Alabama she'd mentioned before. The officers took both of their statements and asked if Cruz could prove that he was the boy's godfather. Since he had Derrick christened, that wouldn't be a problem. He stated to the officers that he and his fiancé would take custody of Lil D. Hollyn looked at her brother with the first smile he'd seen on her since arriving.

After the officers left, Hollyn questioned Cruz on why he'd never told her about Jennifer. Cruz glanced down at his sister and simply stated, "I had everything under control. Besides, what would you have done Hollyn? You and Jennifer weren't friends anymore." Hollyn was curious about this fiancé he spoke of. She looked him up and down, "And since when do you have a fiancé?" she stated. Cruz pulled the small black box out of his pants pocket; his thumb stroked the velvet material while glancing towards the house. "Actually I don't have a fiancé yet, I planned to ask Shawnee over brunch but that as you can see never happened. So if she accepts my proposal or not after today, I have a responsibility to keep with Lil D."

Hollyn sucker punched her brother again and raced into the house, still holding the little black box in her hand. Cruz caught up to her just a moment too late. Shawnee looked at the pair of them disbelievingly that they could be so jovial after what had just transpired. Before she could chastise the pair, Hollyn shoved the closed box in her face. Cruz slumped in the chair deflated. He'd render his control over to the woman who'd stolen his heart six years ago.

Dangerous Curves

I can be your fairytale, your knight in shining armor. I can fulfill your dreams. Your every wish is my command. With Love always, Cruz.

You know how when you were a little girl and you believed in fairy tales, the fantasy of what your life would be; a white dress and prince charming who would carry you away to a château on a hill. You would lie in bed at night with closed eyes with complete and utter faith. Santa Claus, the Tooth Fairy, and Prince Charming were so real you could taste them, but eventually you grow up, and one day you open your eyes only to realize fairy tales are not real. Is there really such a thing as happily ever after? Shawnee reread the note Cruz left in her bag over and over. Shawnee never believed much in fairytales, she knew in her heart there was no such thing. Relationships take work, honesty, communication and most of all trust. She glanced at the man lying beside her and wondered whether she had made the right choices. Could a happy ending really be hers?

The last five days had gone by in a flash. On a whim she showed up at Cruz's condo and she has been there ever since. She promised Hollyn that she would go with her to Jennifer's room to help collect the rest of Lil D's things. Shawnee placed the note on the nightstand beside the bed and adjusted herself under the weight of Cruz's arm. Closing her eyes, she let the sound of the ceiling fan lull her to sleep.

When she awoke the next morning, Cruz had placed tray of fresh fruit, turkey bacon and eggs, with yogurt and juice on the nightstand. Feeling famished, Shawnee grabbed the tray, and adjusting herself she devoured a slice of bacon while reading his note.

You've been so magnificent the last few days; I thought you should sleep in. I'm taking Lil D over to mom's house for the day while I finalize the memorial plans for Jennifer. Enjoy your breakfast my Angel, Love Cruz.

The sun was emerging on the balcony; Shawnee finished off her breakfast and flipped the television on to CNN. Removing the tray from her lap she heard the vibration of her cellphone. Retrieving the phone from the nightstand Shawnee walked out on the balcony. The message changed her mood instantly. The picture was a familiar sight; she saw it several times before. Conversely, seeing it this morning didn't bring her any pleasure.

"Hello?"

"Good Morning beautiful." His voice vibrated through the phone, down her ear canal and spread through her chest. The explosive beating of her heart secreted down her spine and sent shivers to her clitoris.

"Why are you calling me?" Shawnee replied choosing to ignore her screaming body parts.

"I've missed my Sweet Caramel Delight!" he replied.

"Really, I guess that is why I haven't heard from you in months, right?"

"I sent you several messages, Mon Amour. Have you checked your email lately?"

"Oh, I broke my computer." Shawnee stated. "I'm saving up to get a MAC."

"Come to me, mi amour. Votre sourire est mon lever du soleil, votre baiser est mon crépuscule. J'ai besoin de votre amour pour briller à côté de moi. Mon amour."

"So not fair, Malik. Playing the language card."

"Shawnee, falto ao seu gosto. Venha-me. Deixe-me lambê-lo até o seu fluxo de sucos." "Come to me, my love. I need to see you again." Malik stated.

"Where?"

"Mandarin Oriental."

"Do you know how long it would take me to get to Buckhead?" Shawnee stated feeling a bit aggravated.

"My car is at the airport. I'll give you an hour; my driver will be waiting on you."

There was something about Malik that made Shawnee weak in the knees. It wasn't just his killer body that even tailored and stylish suits couldn't hide. His rugged and handsome features exuded power. His obsidian eyes offset his rich brown complexion. A shiver of pure, amatory awareness filled her entire body as she reminisced on their last encounter.

⁊⁊⁊⁊⁊⁊⁊⁊⁊⁊⁊⁊

Shawnee observed herself in the full length mirror. She changed her outfit twice, not wanting too provocative. She settled on a low cut carrot colored blouse and dark blue denim jeans. She completed her ensemble with a pair of matching wedge heels, giving her short frame some height. Satisfied with her wardrobe selection, Shawnee fluffed her curls and added hint of lip gloss. Glancing back at the wall clock, she had less than twenty minutes to get to Hartsfield Airport. Picking up her phone off the nightstand, the black velvet box caught her eye. Shawnee stood frozen in place momentarily. She should have declined to meet Malik. Technically, she wasn't engaged yet so what harm would seeing an old friend cause she mused while staring at the ring box. Telling herself it's just brunch, Shawnee retrieved her keys and purse and headed out.

Arriving at Hartsfield Airport, Malik's driver was waiting on her just as he promised. Shawnee stepped into the town car as he open the door. Settling into the sleek interior, the familiar ringtone began to play. Palpitations in her chest made her pause temporarily before answering.

"Hey baby, did you enjoy your breakfast?" Cruz asked.

"Yes I did, thank you."

"Are you still at the condo? I'm almost finished with

everything and I was going to pick up some lunch before heading back."

"I left about twenty minutes ago, I…I'm… um heading out to meet a friend before I get together with Hollyn later."

"Is everything ok?"

"Yes… yeah, can you pick me up from Hollyn's later this evening? I decided to catch the Marta since I might have a drink or two."

"Anything for you my love. Call me when you are ready."

"Ok, bye!" Shawnee replied hastily. She wanted to end the call before anymore untruths spilled out. Theoretically she wasn't lying, but she wasn't telling the whole truth either.

Malik was clad in his favorite towel sarong, in his favorite spot on the balcony sipping Hennessey Black on the rocks. It has been more than two months since he last saw Shawnee, two very long months. He had no idea he would miss her so much. He hated not having contact with her, hence the reason he cut his trip short. He wanted to feel her warmth and savor the essence of her. He stared out at the downtown scenery knowing momentarily she would be in his embrace. Adjusting the towel around his waist, he took another swig from his glass and headed back inside the house.

The afternoon sun poured out, radiating off the asphalt as Shawnee stepped out of the town car downtown. Feeling the scorching waves caress her face, she adjusted her sunglass and hurriedly walked into the lobby. Standing in the elevator for a moment, Shawnee contemplated her decision to come and see Malik. She closed her eyes and remembered the last time they were together; his bare torso, the sun gleaming off his bald head, and the softness of his lips. When Malik stared into her eyes, he made her feel as if no other woman existed. When they ventured out, he catered to her every need. Malik would never look at other women in front of her. She tried him on several occasions by pointing to other strikingly beautiful women.

He simply stated he didn't need to look at other beautiful women because he had the most beautiful of them all. Mostly, she remembered the feel of his manhood pressed against her through his jeans. Her heart started to expound rapidly in her chest at the images bouncing around in her head. She exhaled audibly and her body quivered at the memory. Before she succumbed to her desire for Cruz, Malik had been her on again off again lover. She refused to embark on anything more than sexual encounters with him due to their conflicting schedules. Malik traveled relentlessly with his job and driving was her escape from the pressures of life. The ding of the elevator brought her back to reality. Shawnee fumbled apprehensively with her attire, she knew she had to remain firm in her approach with Malik. Shawnee sighed, shaking the images from her head. "Just keep it short and sweet," she repeated to herself. Reaching the penthouse suite Shawnee inhaled, exited the elevator, and glanced around the suite. She noticed the orchids sitting on table with her name attached to the card. The room, otherwise, was basic. Standing in the foyer, Shawnee was amazed there were no candles lite, rose petals covering the floor, no soft music, no candy. Just orchids sitting on the table top. She wrestled with the urge of turning around and exiting the room. Backing towards the door, Malik stepped into the foyer stopping her in her tracks. Looking like a deer caught in head lights, she stood there taking in every magnificent cut his abs offered. He added a new tattoo across the right side of his chest. Shawnee stared at the intricate design: the barbed wire heart encased by flames held a solitary letter "S" in the middle. She was in awe that he tattooed his chest. His flawless chest was one of his best features. His nipples when glistened with oil reminded her of a chocolate drop.

Tilting her head sideways, her tongue sliding across his areola's making circular paths making their way to his nipple.

Shawnee heard R. Kelly playing faintly as visions of Cruz replaced the current vision. Shawnee blinked several times as Malik's voice and Derrick's face combined in her mind. "I've missed you, Mon Amour." Startled by the vision and the voice tickling her ear, she jumped as reality set in. No music was playing just the distant sound of the television on CNN. Malik walking up the foyer closing the distance between them. Embracing her, Malik kissed Shawnee's forehead down to her lips.

"I've missed you, Shawnee!"

"Really, I can't tell Malik, usually there's a lot more fluff than just my favorite flowers."

"You just arrived Mon Amour, believe me before you leave there will be no doubt on how much I've missed you."

"I'm not staying, I can't, I have a prior engagement and I...I," Shawnee stumbled over her words before Malik cut her off. She wasn't sure what she wanted to say. Yes she slept with Derrick and had been there with him and Lil D ever since. Still she felt unsure if she would remain. Her vacation would be over shortly and she knew all too well, out of sight meant out of mind. Could Derrick remain faithful once she hit the road again. Before she could continue her thoughts Malik scooped her up and walked into the master room of the suite.

"Malik, I'm with Cruz now." She blurted out.

"The stalker?" Malik questioned.

"He's not the stalker Malik! Cruz... I mean Derrick owns his own business and he drives occasionally. I ran into him before I came up for my home time break. After I got back, I went to see him. Things have changed Malik. He has real feelings for me." Shawnee stated matter of factly.

"What about YOUR feelings? Do you love him? Or Me?"

Shawnee fidgeted with her clothes, stood and turned to face the balcony. She grabbed the remote laying on the bed and flipped through a couple of channels.

"Arrêtez-le Shawnee! Answer me."

"I have to go Malik. I only came to tell you that I am with Derrick now. And to see how you've been." She stated not wanting to look at him.

Turning around, Shawnee walked over to Malik;

placing her hand directly on his tattoo, she kissed him tenderly on the lips and walked toward the door. Malik stood frozen in place until she was almost to the door. This was something so new to him. Shawnee had never turned him down for anything, now she was walking out of his life. Malik snapped back to reality as the click of the door caught his attention. Malik opened the bureau, quickly snatching a pair of jeans and the special box he'd prepared to give Shawnee over dinner. Racing out the room, Malik headed towards the stairs. He knew Shawnee would go straight to his driver and planned to catch them before they pulled off.

Shawnee stepped off the elevator just as Malik came bursting out the side door. The commotion caused everyone in the lobby to turn toward the sound of the clanging door.

"Shawnee, Wait!" Malik bellowed across the room.

Surprised at her name echoing through the lobby, Shawnee spun around to see a shirtless Malik sprinting towards her.

"I can't let you leave without speaking my mind. I know what you said, but give me a moment please, Shawnee." Malik pleaded.

"Fine Malik, what is so urgent you had to race down here like a mad man?"

"When my grandmother was alive, she used to tell me that every time God creates a soul in heaven, he creates another to be its special mate. And that once we're born we begin to search for our soul mate, the one person who's the perfect fit for our mind and body. Shawnee you've been that person for me. I knew it from the very first time I saw you. I've been resisting the very thing I need. I promise you, no one could love you more than me. Take this and only open it if you are ready to be loved like never before. Amei-o toda a minha vida, até antes de que eu o tenha encontrado. A parte dele não foi até você ... ele foi a promessa de reunir a minha alma. Case-se comigo Shawnee."

"English, Malik! Playing the language card is not going to work!" Shawnee seethed.

"I loved you all my life, even before I met you. Part of it wasn't even you… it was the promise of reconnecting my soul. Marry me Shawnee."

Shawnee couldn't believe her ears. She relished all the time spent with Malik, he made her at times feel like no other person existed. Right now everything seemed to move in slow motion. Staring into the eyes of a man she'd known for years, the earth titled on its axis beckoning to Shawnee. She peered down at the mahogany octagon shaped box, her thumb tracing the familiar engraved words atop. Opening her mouth to speak, Shawnee couldn't find the words she wanted to say. In less than two weeks, she received proposals from two men. Incapable of forming a full sentence, Shawnee pushed open the elegant box. Everything moved in slow motion as the lid opened up. The bright lights in the lobby seemed to crash into the three carat heart shaped ruby ring encased in black gold. Shawnee had never seen a ruby illuminate off of sunlight like a flashing red traffic light. Anxiously, Malik stood there awaiting a response from Shawnee. Looking up at her, he couldn't wait any longer. Malik clutched Shawnee in his embrace, closed the space between them and fervently kissed Shawnee. Malik poured every ounce of his being into kissing Shawnee. Frightened by his intense passion, Shawnee pushed away from him and raced out the door.

Meanwhile on the other side of town....

Derrick arrived back at his parents' house after he completed the arrangements for Jen's memorial. He wanted to spend a little alone time with Shawnee. He knew she had plans with Hollyn so he assumed she would be available for lunch. They had barely talked about his impending proposal since Jennifer's untimely appearance and suicide. He shared with her the circumstances that led up to her giving birth to Lil D and the responsibility he assumed by accepting to become the child's god-father. Never did he think he would have to honor that commitment. He assumed Jen had gotten her life together.

Walking back into the house, Cruz slouched into the chair across from his mother. A quick scan of the room and he found Lil D sitting in a familiar little seat concentrating hard, his thick brows were furrowed almost touching. Derrick stared at him before turning his attention back to his mother sitting across from him.

"How did everything go, son?"

"Everything is everything, Mom." Derrick replied. "The arrangements are all set, the memorial will be grave side tomorrow evening. Shawnee and Hollyn are supposed to pick up the rest of his things this afternoon."

"Where is Shawnee, I thought for sure she would be with you." Mrs. Black stated.

"She had something to do today, Mom. I was hoping to meet her for lunch, but she was still out. And before you ask, No we haven't discussed anything yet. Things have just been a little too hectic."

Before he could finish his statement, Lil D raced into the room. Excitement etched across his face, he jumped into Derrick's lap with his paper in hand. Derrick wrapped his arms around him and ran his hands over his head.

"Looks like somebody is in need of a haircut." Derrick stated.

"What did you draw?" Mrs. Black interrupted.

Lil D smiled at Derrick before scooting off his lap and bounding over to Mrs. Black. "I drew you a picture." He announced joyously. Holding up the picture, he began pointing at the various people scattered about the page. "This is me, this is my God daddy D. This is my mommy going to heaven to be with my Grand momma and Grandpa. This is Mr. B. This is my God daddy's friend, I don't remember her name and this is you, my new Grand momma." Lil D stated proudly.

"Well who is this?" Mrs. Black asked pointing to the wildest person on the page.

"That's the mean lady that fought with my mommy. I don't like her." Lil D said.

Mrs. Black let out a chuckle. She's not really mean

son, she stated sweetly. She just had a misunderstanding with your Mom. Let me show you. Mrs. Black reached behind her and picked up the album off couch table. She flipped through several pages until her eyes landed on the picture she was searching for. Leaning forward, she placed the photo album on his lap. Look at these, this is a picture of Hollyn and Jennifer at their eighth graduation. This one here is their Sweet 16 slumber party. And over here is their high school graduation. This is your mom. This is Hollyn.

"This looks like my mommy, but she never smiles." He stated.

"Your mom used to smile all the time. Her smile looked exactly like yours." Hollyn interjected. She walked in while he studied the pictures of the two of them together. Lil D, scooted closer to Mrs. Black as the sound of Hollyn's voice drew closer to him. He was still unsure of her. He skimmed her face and then looked back at the picture of his mom and her at the sweet 16 party. Hollyn walked over and sat at the far end of the couch. She pulled her hair up and unbuckled the gold necklace that always hung around her neck. She placed it on the table before speaking.

"See that picture there, this necklace was our present to each other."

"My mommy gave me a necklace like that, she said to always keep it with me and she would always be around." Lil D stated, pulling the gold chain from his pocket.

Hollyn began to cry, she recognized the gold heart that her once best friend had worn. Her sobs startled Lil D, for a moment. Curiously, he went to look at the necklace she placed on the table. After inspecting the necklace on the table and the one he held in his hand. He pushed the two hearts together, picked them both up and patted Hollyn on the knee.

"It's okay, don't cry. My mommy said she was going to be with her Mommy and Daddy. Don't cry, don't cry, okay." Lil D said, patting her knee.

Hollyn wiped the tears from her eyes and scooped Lil D in her arms. Hollyn sat rocking back and forth with Lil D in her arms.

Shawnee and Hollyn arrived at the rooming house where Jennifer lived. Hollyn had previously called the manager the day before to make sure that it would be okay to retrieve what little odds and ends Jennifer had left. Upon arriving, they were greeted by the manager who informed them he needed to rent the room.

"All of Jennifer's things are in this box." He said, handing the box to Hollyn. "Oh before I forget, Jennifer brought me a letter to give to you. Hold on it's in the office." Moments later the manager returned and handed Hollyn a sealed envelope with her name on the front. She recognized the curly letters and arrows. Hollyn started to tremble, she flipped the envelope over looking for Jennifer's signature tag. Hollyn's knees began to buckle at the sight of Jennifer's tag on the back of the envelope. She tried to remain strong, inhaling and taking deep breathes wasn't keeping the tears at bay. As Hollyn's grief took over, the apartment manager and Shawnee ushered her back inside the car.

そうそうそうそうそうそうそう

Dear Jolly Holly,

If you are reading this that means, life's issues has gotten the best of me. I want to start off by saying I've really missed my friend, my sister. Life really took a turn after high school. I've wished many, many times to go back to before graduation. You know they say hindsight is 20/20. If I had it to do all over again. I would and the main thing I would change is my silence. Holly, the rumors that you heard were not true. I didn't sleep with Bryce and I never set him up. After you left early to go to school, I went out a couple of times with Sade and her crew but they were so wild. Hollyn, you know we never did any drugs. And the one time we snuck some alcohol from your brother's stash we barely drank one cup. When I arrived at Sade's house Bryce was already there. I had nothing to do with it. When you stopped talking to me, my world slowly started to fall apart. Then my parents were killed and I needed my friend. I came to your school. But I was so afraid we would get into another fight that I didn't want to embarrass you. I know, you came to the funeral and stayed with me afterwards. I should've tried harder. We were sisters. Best Friends Forever. Of all the things I lost over the years, the one thing that I held onto was our necklace. I gave it to my son. I know who his father is and I don't think he should. Malcolm Ballo is not a decent man. I thought I was in love, but he discarded me like day old trash and left me with those monsters. I am pretty sure that Cruz has told you all what happened that night. He said he would help me, but I just couldn't get pass it. I miss my Jolly Holly. Please help Cruz with Lil D. He tries to be a big man, but his just a baby boy. Everything you'll need for Lil D is in this envelope. I've written him a letter and had a talk with him already. I know Cruz will teach him how to be a man,

regardless of the way he came to be. I love you Hollyn. I hope
you will forgive me someday. Love always, Jennifer.

જ⁄જ⁄જ⁄જ⁄જ⁄જ⁄જ⁄જ⁄જ⁄જ⁄જ⁄

Hearing the name Ballo sparked Shawnee's attention reminding her of her unfinished business with Malik. Waiting for Hollyn to regain her composure, Shawnee instructed the driver to return back to the Black's house.

Shawnee wasn't the only one listening to Hollyn read Jennifer's letter. Instantly the driver's palms became sweaty and beads of perspiration formed on his balding head. He quickly slipped his phone out of his coat pocket and snapped a couple shots of the two. Before taking this news to Malcom, he knew he would need some evidence. He would definitely need to hear more of this conversation. Glancing down at his watch, he took a quick detour that landed right where he needed to be, downtown Atlanta traffic.

Shawnee spoke softly, "Hollyn you can't let the guilt consume you. I can't imagine what it feels like to see your former friend kill herself. But you have to forgive yourself, she did."

"I'm a horrible person, she offered an olive branch and I threw it back. I wasn't ready to forgive and forget. I believed what I saw in the pictures, I just should've listened. I always told myself that I had time, I didn't even care how bad things had gotten for her." Hollyn mumbled.

"Hollyn, you are not horrible, sweetie. What you have to realize is both of you made a mistake. Communication is the key to correcting those mistakes. Someone once told me, 'Tomorrow is the most horrible assumption'. So stop beating yourself up over what you should've or could've done better. Honor your friend by granting her request. Cruz will need your help with Lil D. Besides, if this Malcom person reappears he could lay claim to Lil D." Shawnee stated.

"I never looked at it that way, Shawnee. Thank you,"

Hollyn stated.

"No problem. Now, who is Malcolm Ballo and who was Bryce?" Shawnee questioned.

"Bryce was the guy I dated during high school. After I left early for college, I was sent pictures of Him and Hollyn in bed. Shortly after that, he was killed by a stray bullet. I hated Jennifer for sleeping with him and never really gave her a chance to explain. Anytime he was brought up I changed the subject or left. Looking back now, I guess I should have."

Noticing that the car wasn't moving Shawnee rolled down the driver's window, "What's going on?" She asked.

"Sorry ma'am, there was a detour and now it looks like an accident up ahead." He said.

"After you drop us off, please let Malik know I will return tomorrow; there's just too much going on today." Shawnee instructed.

"Yes ma'am."

Turning her attention back to Hollyn, her face scrunched up staring at a torn picture. Reflecting for a moment, Shawnee stared out the window. She thought about the name, Ballo. There was only one other person she knew with that name. Malik.

Hollyn stared at the picture. She dreaded the upcoming memorial service. she took a deep breath, praying that she could remain in control. The picture she held in her hand, reminded her of the smiling girl she had been close friends with once upon a time. Turning the picture over, she stared at the familiar hand writing. 'Malcom and me Six Flags'.' Who the hell is Malcom? Hollyn murmured.

"Good question. I was just about to ask you the same thing." Shawnee stated.

"I certainly have no idea, I'll get Cruz to check it out." Hollyn stated.

"Wait…Shawnee blurted out. I mean hold off on asking Cruz. I have a few connections of my own. I'll check into it after the memorial service."

Finally arriving back at the Black's house, Hollyn and Shawnee exited the car. To their surprise they were greeted cheerfully by Lil D, who leaped into Hollyn's open embrace. Pulling away from the curb, the driver's jaw dropped as he eyed the little boy who could very well be Malcom's son. He quickly snapped a couple of shots as Hollyn slipped him back to the ground. He saved the photos, before sending a quick text to Malcolm.

By the time they arrived back at the condo, both Cruz and Shawnee were spent. The day's turn of events had Shawnee still baffled about Malcolm Ballo, Lil D's potential father. She prayed it was nothing, but the feeling in her gut told her that Malik's sudden proposal was not just a coincidence anymore.

A few hours after the memorial service Shawnee excused herself from the Black's house, she opted to drive herself up instead of meeting the driver at the airport. She felt the ride up would give her the much needed time to think about the events that transpired previously. Arriving at the hotel, Shawnee had gone over in her head what she wanted to say several times. Making love to Cruz the night before helped to solidify what she believed as fate. She would return his ring and find out if he knew who Malcom was.

Shawnee knocked on the door awaiting his handsome self to answer. She was still mulling over what she wanted to say to him, and was ready to lay it all on the line. Malik answered the door and his appearance gave Shawnee more questions than she cared to have at the moment. She was so ready to let this be the end all be all. However, one look at Malik's swollen bandaged lower lip and badly bruised cheek banished all of Shawnee's earlier musings. Stepping back from the open door, she narrowed her eyes at Malik, both alarmed and confused by his mangled appearance.

"Oh my god! Were you in an accident?" she asked.

"No I wasn't in an accident, but something just as bad, if not worse," he replied taking her into his embrace.

"Do you need to go to the hospital?

"All I need now is for nurse Shawnee to grace me with some tender loving care." He cocked his head sideways, giving Shawnee his best impression of puppy eyes he could muster. "I can't do much kissing until the swelling goes down." He ran his tongue over his upper lip and adopted a duck face expression. The pain made him wince slightly at his comical expression.

"Stop joking, Malik. This looks serious!" Shawnee

exclaimed. "What in the world happened? When I left here yesterday you were fine. Now in less than a day you're bruised up? Spill it, Malik! Now!" Shawnee ordered.

Instead of answering, Malik reached up and pulled Shawnee down beside him and wrapped her in his arms. Cuddling her in a protective embrace, he sighed letting her know how relieved he was to have her in his arms. With one hand pressed to the side of her head, he nudged her cheek against his neck. She could feel the beat of his heart as if it were pounding in his neck instead of his chest. He drew in a couple deep breaths and their bodies moved in sync with each other as he took a moment to compose himself.

"I got into a fight last night outside of a sports bar." He finally said easing back to get a look in her face.

"Did you call the police?" Shawnee gasped, rising up. She tried to pull out of Malik's embrace, but he tightened his grip not letting her go.

"It's not as bad as it looks, really, my brother looks

worse than I do." He stated. "Please stay with me tonight. It was a hellava night and I need you Shawnee."

"Why are you fighting with your brother? Would his name happen to be Malcom?" She inquired.

"It's a long story. I'd rather not go into right now." Malik stated.

Shawnee sucked her teeth in dissatisfaction and scowled at Malik.

"Stay with me a while, Mon Armor. It's been a long, long day. I've barely seen you since I arrived." Malik pleaded.

Hesitantly, Shawnee nodded. Pulling her back down onto his bed, Malik was temporarily satisfied. They sat in silence for hours then finally drifted off to sleep. Shawnee stirred restless against Malik. Her butt pressing against his stomach awakened him, giving a stiff hard on. Shawnee stretched slightly causing her rear end to rise and fall against his swollen penis as she settled in even closer. Malik clenched his teeth in torment as a devilish grin played over his lips. He loved the way her body felt next to his. This was a moment he wanted to cherish untainted. Sliding himself closer to mold his body further into hers, his move initiated a shift against his well primed member. Shawnee felt the rise against her behind and began to grind her ass in circular motion. She let out a soft moan as Malik placed his hook between her ass cheeks. Feeling the curvature of his manhood, Shawnee jumped up realizing she was still in the arms of Malik and not Cruz as she had been dreaming. Grabbing her cell phone she realized although it was close to midnight, it wasn't nearly as late as she thought.

"I... I... I... I've got to go, Malik. Cruz is waiting for me." She stammered.

"Wait! What kinda man let's his woman go for hours without one single call?" Malik asked. "While you've been here with me, he hasn't called or texted you at all. Just like you are here with me, he's off with someone else. When are you gonna wake up Shawnee? I love you, Mon Armor. I proposed to you and have yet to get an answer. What has he done?" Malik asked.

Heading out the door, Shawnee replied, "That doesn't matter and it's not your concern what Cruz is doing. I'll see you tomorrow. I've gotta get home." Shawnee closed the door and raced out to the elevator.

Forty-five minutes later, Shawnee arrived back at the condo. Cruz had left her a couple messages inquiring where she was, when she would return, and that Lil D. was spending the night with his mother and Hollyn. Walking into the condo, she found him sprawled out on the bed half naked. Quickly removing her clothes, Shawnee took her place next to him. Spooning her body to fit next to his, she wedged her leg between his. Relaxing, she luxuriated in the glorious rush of happiness that flowed through her. She was in bliss. Satisfied with the life Cruz was offering, Shawnee knew that she would have to return the exquisite ring Malik had proposed to her with.

Feeling her body next to his Cruz sighed, wrapped his arm around her body, hugged her tight, and pulled her closer to him.

Shawnee reached back with and claimed his arousal. Cruz tensed. He whispered in her ear, "That's a lethal weapon there. I hope you're ready, it's locked and loaded."

"I sure hope so," Shawnee whispered, massaging the length with short, tight strokes. Cruz moaned at each upward squeeze. His entire being was on fire, surging with a fierce desire to possess Shawnee like never before. He slid his hands up her legs searching for the edge of her panties only to find she wasn't wearing any. Snaking his fingers up the small patch of pubic hair, he raked the softness with tender strokes. Moving his hands along her folds gently making his way to her clitoris, he increased his stroking from a slow roll to rapid back and forth motions that caused a low moan to escape her mouth. Shawnee arched her back and spread her thighs allowing Cruz to take advantage of the opening and plunge two fingers deep inside her sensuous and slippery core.

Taking his tongue, he slowly traced the slopes of

Shawnee's shoulder. He placed languid licks on the tender flesh at the nape of her neck into the soft spot behind her ear, adoring the taste of her natural skin. An instant thunderbolt of electric shock shivered down his spine as Shawnee moaned, "Oh baby don't stop, that feels so good." Her sensual sounds intensified their emotional connection; making him even hornier and hungrier for her than when he first awakened with her beside him.

Shawnee maintained her steady grip on his rock hard shaft as she slid around to face him. With puckered lips she placed kisses over his face before sliding her tongue down his nipples, suckling both before leaving a trail of fire down his chest.

"Damn baby… Damn!" Cruz moaned when her lips seized the tip of his erection.

He made an upward thrust of his hips, pushing himself half-way into her mouth while looking down upon her head buried in the dark triangle between his legs. Her hand job had primed Cruz and now here he was at the point of explosion with each stroke of her tongue. She sucked and tugged, licked and squeezed his tool with expert precision, applying just right amount of pressure countered by relief as she stimulated him beyond his wildest imagination. Just when she brought him to a thundering climax, she pulled away and delivered a cool stream of air onto his flaming flesh. He loved this erotic side of her. Her sexy moves and seductive manipulations had him addicted. Shawnee was the woman he would never tire of loving and even though she had him literally by the balls he wasn't complaining.

"This feels so good," he mused, loving Shawnee's ability to sense what he wanted and needed. She always delivered with just enough to keep him hungry for more of her. Her attention to his needs solidified his belief that what they had together was very special, extremely natural, and meant to last. He waited a very long time for a woman to make him feel complete and with Shawnee he found that. He planned to do everything in his power to satisfy and love her forever.

Shawnee's sensual manipulation increased, so did his

urgency. Refusing to give up his seed and ruin their erotic ride, he allowed her to bring him to the brink of eruption once more before compressing.

Gently he caressed her beneath her chin; guiding her upwards, he smiled lovingly at her as he looked forward to satisfying her every need.

Cruz guided Shawnee onto him, spread her knees on either side, and made slow sweeping motions on her inner thighs as she settled down and accepted his penetration into her wetness. He traced the outside of her nipples before suckling on each.

Looking into her face, he melted under the tender caressing gaze through fire lit eyes charged with seductive energy of their intimate connection. Like a tiger that had captured its prey, she peered through his soul with hungry half-closed eyes that gleamed with intensity assuring him he was doing exactly what she needed. Cruz's heart did a somersault as Shawnee leaned in and pulled his mouth to hers once more. He kissed her lush lips with a passion that scared even him. Like forbidden fruit, her lips tempted him with every escaping moan.

Holding on to her waist, Cruz flipped her over on her back and used both hands to raise her hips off the bed, driving deeply into her with firm urgent strokes. Shawnee threw her head back and claimed his shaft with her wetness pushing him deeper into her tunnel of love. Soft grunts of satisfaction caressed his ears. "This is all I want," she said between moans anchoring her legs around his waist as ecstasy lulled them together.

Cruz pumped steadily, moving in and out delivering slow easy strokes that helped him gain control of his emotions while building momentum to go the distance. He placed one hand over her breast and stroked her nipples with tingling circular motions. Feeling them harden beneath his palm, he continued back and forth, round and round. He played in rhythmic delight as more outburst of husky and lust filled moans escaped her lips.

Reciprocating his attention, Shawnee flattened her

palms against his smooth rippled chest and abs sliding them in an up and down motion. Surrendering to her vibrating need, Cruz slid his hands off her heavy breast and pressed each of them along the soft curves of her stomach. He rocked her forward without withdrawing from her love-slick core. He rested her ass on his upper thighs, helping create a vise-like grip that drew them tighter than before. Yielding to the bursting sensation of uncontrollable joy, he moved into her faster as his urge to release escalated higher.

"Give it to me, give it me," Shawnee gasped, rocking rapidly back and forth.

"It's all yours baby," Cruz replied, shuddering in unspoken passion as a tremor of ecstasy slid through him pushing him into the raging inferno of seduction.

Shawnee swayed, arching her back and presenting luscious nipples that begged for his attention. Cruz took a pointy nipple into his mouth and suckled it until she released a pleasure filled cry. He captured the other and teased her unmercifully as he worked his tongue to get her to that magical point of indescribable pleasure. Shawnee took his hand and placed it between her ass cheeks until he reached her wetness then pulled it back towards her forbidden hole. He slid his fingers in slow back and forth motions gently until he felt her vagina walls pulsing again snatching his manhood. As his finger entered her anal cavity in search of the hidden g-spot, Shawnee let out a searing cry of impending climax. Cruz pulled her securely in his embrace as all restraint peaked in their erotic journey. Arriving simultaneously at their final destination, they held onto each other and drifted off into perfect cessation.

The next morning Shawnee was laying in the middle of the bed with a soft smile on her face. It was still early and she was wide awake. She went to sleep wrapped in Cruz's arms and awakened the same way. Each time they made love it was incredible. He was incredible. She was seeing a different side of Cruz. He was considerate, focused and gentlemanly. Basking in the afterglow, the compression on her bladder beckoned for her attention. Easing out of bed, Shawnee made her way to bathroom. Staring at the post it note on the mirror, a joyous sensation rippled through her body.

"I am going to love you for as long as I live." Cruz

The sun was rising, beautiful hues of blues, oranges and

brilliant reds began to blanket the sky. Shawnee seized the note off glass and sprinted back into the room leaping on top of an unsuspecting Cruz awakening him with kisses.

In one swift move, Cruz reversed their position and nibbled at her neck. He ran his hands down the length of her thighs, caressed her knee before sliding them open. His fingers fluttered across the back side of Shawnee's knee causing her to erupt in laughter.

"Look who's ticklish." Cruz chided swiping his hand once again over the same spot. Shawnee bucked and squirmed try to free herself from his encirclement.

"Where do you think you are going?" Cruz taunted.

Between bouts of laughter and squeals, Shawnee gasped, "Away from you!"

"Oh no, you're mine now baby." Cruz stated, leaning in he kissed her passionately. "I'll stop for now under one condition," he said.

Catching a breath, Shawnee replied, "Anything,

anything."

"Say you'll be my wife." Cruz replied.

"I don't know?" Shawnee stated.

"Wrong answer," Cruz replied and commenced his assault once again on Shawnee.

"Marry me Shawnee," Cruz asked. "I promise with every breath I breathe to be your protector, your provider, your comforter."

Looking into his eyes, she felt his passion radiate with every word. She knew he wasn't just tormenting her with the tickling.

"You don't think we are moving too fast?" Shawnee asked

"I feel like I've loved you forever. No other woman has ever made me feel as complete… as whole." Cruz replied.

Scooting back on her elbows, Shawnee beheld the man before her. Shawnee reached out and stroked his nape gently. "Will you love me when I am old and gray, when my titties hang damn near to my navel, when I've gained weight or have false teeth?"

Cruz couldn't help but burst into laughter at Shawnee's question. She folded her arms across her chest and puckered her lips attempting her best pout.

"Don't be like that, my sweet. You've gotta admit, that was funny. But to answer your question, YES! I'll gum you to death when my warrior can't rise." Cruz stated.

"Since you put it that way, Yes, I'll marry you!" Shawnee replied.

Cruz buried his face into Shawnee's neck and breathed in her essence. She felt his heart pounding as he wrapped her in his embrace. It seemed like hours had passed instead of mere minutes when Shawnee broke their embrace. She informed Cruz that although she agreed to marry him, she still had a job. Cruz sat back eyeing Shawnee. He wanted to tell her to quit her job. She didn't need to work being his wife would be job enough. He didn't want her to leave his side. Yet knowing her, he felt telling her to quit would cause strife that they didn't need right away. Cruz was certain he should let her decide. Breaking the silence, Shawnee spoke first.

"I know what you're thinking." She stated.

"Oh really, you're a mind reader now?" Cruz asked.

"No, but it's written all over your face. You don't want me to drive anymore. I can't not work. But we can compromise. I've got to make a run to Savannah in two days. So let's just enjoy this time. When I return we can work something out." Shawnee stated.

"I suppose that will have to do." Cruz replied. "I've got some running around to do and I have to check on 'lil D. What do you have planned for the day?"

Looking away from Cruz, Shawnee fiddled with her hair. Lying wasn't one of her strong suits. And lying to Cruz's face wasn't right. "I've got some loose ends to tie up and then I thought I'd invite Hollyn to lunch since I'll be gone for a few days." Shawnee replied.

Shawnee reluctantly eased from the bed, and headed towards the bathroom. Standing in the door frame she looked back at Cruz who seemed deep in thought. A wave of uneasiness crossed over her and she returned to where Cruz sat staring out towards the balcony. Walking into his space, she lifted his hand and tugged him into a standing position. She gazed up into his chocolate eyes, lowered her voice and gave her best Teddy P impression, "Let's take a shower... shower together... I'll wash your body... you'll wash mine. Yeah."

Smiling like a Cheshire cat, Cruz responded quickly, "You ain't gotta ask me twice. Let's go!"

Shawnee entered the parking lot where she kept her truck during layovers. Hastening around to the back of the vehicle, she bent over, grabbed her bag, and slammed the trunk closed. When she turned around, she stopped and shrieked. A man was standing there blocking her path and he didn't look as if he planned on moving.

"Come with me," he ordered, pulling Shawnee by the shoulder and snatching her bag away from her. Taking hold of her arm, he twisted into her back and forced her toward a black van with heavily tinted windows that was parked alongside the truck stop.

The side door of the van slid open. The man threw her bag inside. Shawnee struggled to get free, but he gripped her harder and pushed her headfirst into the dark vehicle. With her face pressed to the floor, he straddled her. Using a roll of duct tape, he quickly bound her hands and feet. When he rose, Shawnee flipped over and used her bound feet to kick at him.

"Stay still Bitch!" he yelled, shoving her back with a slap

across the face. Grabbing her by her ponytail, he yanked her face towards his. "Try anything and I'll beat the living shit outta you!" He pulled at her hair so hard, Shawnee thought he would snatch it out of the root as he pushed her hard against the van floor.

A surge of pain ripped through Shawnee's head as her temple connected with the metal bar where the seats had been removed. She let out the loudest high-pitched scream she could manage; praying someone would hear her and realize she was in trouble.

"You'd better shut up, you stupid bitch!" A familiar voice barked from over the front seat.

Surprised, Shawnee rocked, raising herself off the floor, as the van squealed out of the parking lot. It was dark inside the van, she could see the driver through the rearview mirror, the sight of him made her gasp.

It can't be, Shawnee thought as her eyes connected with those of Malik's driver, Rasheed.

"Rasheed, what are you doing? Where is Malik?"

"Just shut up and cooperate," Rasheed bellowed in a tone that sent shivers down Shawnee's spine. She never heard the usually cordial driver speak like this.

"If you want to see your boyfriend again you'd better shut the fuck up and stay down on the floor!" Rasheed barked.

"My boyfriend?" Shawnee repeated. She grasped for answers as the van sped through traffic. Her thoughts ran together as Rasheed took one sharp turn after another. Her mind quickly drifted back to the last time she saw Malik all bruised in his hotel room. *What had he gotten her into? Why was she being kidnapped?*

"What does this have to do with Malik?" she questioned, refusing to sit back and remain silent.

"Didn't I say shut the fuck up?" Rasheed yelled, before glancing at the man in the passenger seat. "Shut her up!" he ordered.

The man who taped her up reached back and swung forcefully at her barely missing her face as she scoot further back inside the van. Rasheed tossed the man his phone and told him to take a couple pictures of Shawnee. Pulling out a different phone, Shawnee heard him say, "I got her." Shawnee pulled her knees into her stomach and scoot over towards the metal bar. She noticed the sharp edge near the end of the bar. Facing the back of the driver seat, Shawnee scratched at the edges trying to cut the duct tape holding her arms together. She clamped her teeth down tight to prevent herself from screaming as the metal edge made contact with her skin. Sliding over a little more, Shawnee continued the up and down motion to free her duct taped hands.

Rasheed caught sight of Shawnee's shoulder movement and swerved the van causing her to fall over sideways. Lying there sideways Shawnee tried to calm her nerves down. If she could get control of herself she might be able to think of a way out of this mess. Shawnee slowed her breathing. Taking in deep breaths, she tried to sit up again. Reclaiming a sitting position, Shawnee wriggled her wrist behind her back until she was able to reach her back pockets. Shawnee slid her cell phone up just enough to flip the volume switch to the off position. Feeling a wee bit more confident, Shawnee then slipped the phone out of her pocket, placing it on the floor beside her. Satisfied that her call tones wouldn't ring back, Shawnee pressed the center button and slid her finger across the screen, leaving a trail of blood and bringing the phone to life. Shawnee pressed the keypad, recalling the last person she'd spoken with earlier, Cruz.

"Where are you taking me? What do you plan on doing to me?" Shawnee asked.

"If you don't shut the hell up, I'm going to shut you up myself!" the man replied, eyeing Shawnee suspiciously.

Silence fell over the van as Shawnee slumped back against the wall and tried to think. With the van racing through the street, Shawnee strained to catch glimpses of the highway signs and landmarks she could see. The strange man had hit her so hard, she didn't realize she'd lost a contact out of her eye. Straining to see the signs, Shawnee finally realized they were heading south towards Macon. Deciding it was in her best interest to pretend to cooperate, Shawnee chewed the inside of her lip while trying to keep her nerves in check. The one thing she was sure of was this had something to do with Malik. *What did they want with her,* she pondered.

When the van finally rolled to a stop, Shawnee sat upright and slid her phone back into her pocket. She tried squinting to see if anything looked familiar. Rasheed had parked behind what appeared to be an abandoned warehouse. Snatching up her bag, Rasheed exited the van followed by the burly man who opened the van's side door. He yanked Shawnee out of the van dragging her into one of the worn down buildings.

⌘⌘⌘⌘⌘⌘⌘⌘⌘⌘⌘

Derrick clicked off his phone; he was both, concerned and frustrated. He had been trying to get through to

Shawnee all afternoon with no success. He left several messages and sent a couple texts. He attempted to call her again and got the 'caller was unavailable' message. He was perturbed by this; it wasn't like her to ignore his calls. Something about this whole thing just didn't feel right to him. Picking up his phone, he decided he would dial her once again before dialing Hollyn to see if she heard from her. After briefly speaking with Hollyn, he returned to working on the surveillance equipment he was installing at the front of his store. While he was working, his mind kept drifting to Shawnee. He hoped that her not answering was only related to the compromise she mentioned before leaving. Maybe she was just meeting with her boss to work out the details.

Satisfied that the new security cameras would work well, Derrick prepared to close shop when he noticed the blinking light on the store answering machine. Pressing the replay button, he heard faint scratching sounds in the distance. Replaying the message, he surmised it must've been a wrong number. Erasing the message, he armed the store's security alarm and got into his truck. He tried calling her once again, still no answer. Frustrated, he punched the steering wheel. *Get it together*, he thought. Then remembered he could check her location from the computer since he just linked her device to his. Cruz turned the ignition, accelerated and peeled out of the parking lot. His gut was telling him something just wasn't right about the situation at hand.

Stopping at the red light, Cruz tried to call Shawnee again. No Answer. The car behind him leaned in on his horn forcing him to sit his phone down and drive, frustrated as hell. There had to be a reasonable explanation for her not to answer. Pressing the pedal down, he exceeded the speed limit as he raced to get home.

Back inside the warehouse, Shawnee was relieved of the duct taped cuffs around her legs and hands. She was then ushered to a worn out couch and violently pushed to a seated position. Rasheed retrieved his phone and placed a call. "She's here." He spoke quickly before turning around to Shawnee.

"Speak!" He ordered.

Stunned at the command, Shawnee quickly yelled, "Help! Help me!"

"Where's the boy?" a voiced asked from the speaker. Shawnee was confused at the question, she peered at Rasheed before screaming once again. Barely getting the word out, Rasheed back handed her hard across the face. Shawnee flew back on the couch gripping her face as blood trickled from her nose.

"That's enough." The voice said over the speaker. "I don't need her beat up, Malik still has to have something after handing over my stones." Dazed and confused,

Shawnee set up at hearing Malik's name being mentioned.

"Strip her, secure her and call my dear brother! I'll be there in twenty minutes." He ordered before hanging up the line.

Rasheed pointed to the burly man, "You heard him, strip her and tie her up." He said as he dialed the number into his phone.

Malik had just walked back into his room after taking a swim at the indoor pool when his phone rang. He pressed talk and listened in shock as Rasheed told him exactly what he had to do if he ever wanted to see his precious Shawnee alive again.

"Bring the stones and the money to the Firearms Traders warehouse at 3565 Pio Nino Ave. If you alert the police, she will die! There is a warehouse behind the store. Knock on the side door in one hour."

"I won't bring anything until I know Shawnee is alive. Rasheed, how could you? I treated you like family. If you hurt her, you're dead!" Malik screamed.

"She may be a little bloody, but she's not dead, yet, Malik. Time's a ticking, now you have fifty-five minutes." Rasheed snickered into the phone.

Malik sat stunned for a moment. He assumed Shawnee had already left for her run. How did she end up with Rasheed? Malcom had finally gone too far. He would no longer be his brother's keeper. Walking to the wall safe, Malik turned the dual keys until he heard the familiar clicking sound. Reaching in the safe, Malik pulled out his customized desert eagles, an extra clip, and the old elm box. Flipping the box open, Malik stared at the fifteen stones, the last of his inheritance. Malik carefully placed all the items in his black back pack, secured it with a small lock, and sprinted down the stairs. Once outside, he mounted his Ninja ZX and peeled out of the parking lot. The louder the bike roared the harder his heartbeat, could he really kill his own flesh and blood. Malcom had been living the fast life for far too long. Malik had enough of his drugs, booze, and gambling debts to last a lifetime. Being brought up in the same household under the same influences and rules didn't mean you would turn out the same. Malik had taken advantage of all that migrating to America had to offer. He received a quality education and graduated two years early. After college he enlisted in the Marines and spent four years in Iraq. Following his completed tour, Malik took a job as an international interpreter.

Malik maneuvered the Ninja in and out of traffic along I-75 until he reached Highway 23. He met Malcolm at Firearm Traders before; however, this time would be different. Malik replayed the altercation at the sports bar with Malcolm in his head. Maybe if he'd just given him the cash he asked for Shawnee would not be in peril now. It was all his fault. Now if anything happened to her, he would be forced to choose between the woman he loved and his brother. "There has to be another way," Malik told himself.

The warehouse was dark and filled with rubbish. It reeked of decaying wood and rusted metal. Using the flashlight on his key ring, Malik looked over the place as he strode up the backside of the building. Malik listened intently for sound emitting from the building. It was eerily quiet. *Too quiet,* he thought. *Had Malcom sent him on a wild goose chase so he could vandalize his home,* he pondered. The footsteps reverberating off the hollow walls of the warehouse signaled that they were inside, jolting Malik back to the present.

Moving quickly, he slipped through the back door of the warehouse. Peering around the beam, Malik could see Malcolm standing by the door of the trashed room. He spotted Rasheed sitting at a table. Across the room on a disgustingly filthy couch sat Shawnee, her hands were duct taped and what looked like dried blood was on her face. An unknown man stood beside her. A cold quiver of disgust coursed through his body, despite the heat that engulfed the pungent room. Scanning the warehouse again, Malik needed to be sure there were only three of them there excluding Shawnee. Three against one would not do. Malik snapped his silencer to the Desert Eagle. Lowering his body to the floor, he scurried across the room with the stealth of a ninja.

Arriving at the condo, Cruz still had an uneasy feeling. It was almost ten o'clock and he had yet to hear from Shawnee. Picking up the phone, he dialed Hollyn again.

"Hey sis, did Shawnee call you?" he asked.

"No, but she did say she would meet me down here in Savannah. I'm gonna be down here for a week or so with Kierra." Hollyn replied. "What did you do?"

"What makes you think I did something? I just haven't heard from her since she left this morning." Cruz replied.

"That's not a national emergency you know, bro? If you feel that much concern call her dispatcher like you usually do, or better yet, just activate the find your phone. It'll tell you exactly where she is." Hollyn stated.

"I owe you one!" Derrick said, hanging up the phone and racing over to the computer. Logging into the computer, Derrick accessed the website for the cellular carrier and clicked the link to find my phone. Seconds later, his phone vibrated and the red light flashed on the screen indicating his exact location. Tapping the desk with his fingers, he watched as his mother's line, Lil D's line and finally Shawnee's line blinked on the screen. He knew something was wrong, perspiration began forming on his forehead as he zoomed in on the street finder application. A million thoughts raced through Derrick's brain, but the one that echoed the loudest, *What Shawnee was doing in Macon? Did the truck break down?* Cruz zoomed in closer. The street finder was pretty accurate. Her truck was nowhere in sight. Derrick stood from the computer. Pacing back and forth, he dialed the dispatch office. Maybe they changed her deliver, he mused. Waiting for someone to answer in the office. Cruz walked to his walk-in closet and reached in the top and pulled out the black aluminum box. Turning back around, he placed the box on the desktop, picked up his keys and opened up the box. Inside he pulled out his Glock 19 and concealment papers. Tucking them inside his waistband, he scribbled down the address 3565 Pio Nino Ave and walked out the door.

By the time he made it too I-285, Shawnee's dispatcher had finally informed him that she hadn't shown up for work at all. They had to get the load picked up by someone else. She had been trying to reach her all day as well, without any luck. Her truck was still parked and no one had heard from her at all. That was not the news Cruz wanted to hear. But now he knew something was wrong. Pressing the accelerator to the floor, he pass several cars before rolling up on an unmarked car sitting in the median. Not wanting to incite a high speed chase, he reluctantly slowed his pace to just above the speed limit.

Malik slithered up behind the couch, where Shawnee was bound. Approaching the edge of the couch, he fired two rounds into the burly man standing beside Shawnee. Unaware of what hit him, he crumbled to the floor like the heap of garbage he was. Seeing the man hit the floor, Shawnee's eyes grew bigger as she scurried to the other end of the couch.

"Okay, you wanted to talk? Here I am," Malik boldly announced letting them know he would not be intimidated as he stepped over the mass of man lying dead on the floor. He had gotten Shawnee indirectly involved in this mess and he was going to get her out alive. Even if it meant killing his brother. Malik stood in front of Shawnee; he squatted down, and removed the tape from her mouth.

"It's going to be alright, baby." He said.

Relief swept over Shawnee like a cool autumn breeze. Lifting her to her feet, Malik hugged her tight for a brief moment. With his gun still aimed at Malcolm, he could hear her sobbing cries of relief, feel her heart hammering against his shirt and sense the terror that engulfed her.

"Where are the stones?" Malcolm shouted across the room.

Ignoring the sound of his brother's voice, Malik peered into Shawnee's squinted eyes. "Trust me baby, it's going to be okay. Trust me please!" He stated.

"Get up," Rasheed ordered, forcing Malik to release Shawnee as he felt the point of his gun in his shoulder. Malik turned to face Rasheed and noticed the safety still in the locked position. Malik raised his free hand, and with the other hand he chopped Rasheed in the throat, grabbed his wrist, and spun it around snapping it. The speediness of the move, caused Rasheed to stumble backwards, cradling his wrist while gasping for air. Malik pulled his other Desert Eagle from his back and aimed at Malcolm.

"Don't even think about moving, brother dear," he stated peering at Rasheed.

"Many, many times I told you Rasheed, Money is the root of all evil. You were paid handsomely for your services, yet you still want more the wrong way." Sorry excuse of a man Malik spat.

The searing pain coursed through Rasheed as he lay on the floor staring into the last eyes he would see. "Fuck you, Malik." He slurred.

"Is that your final answer?" Malik questioned. Shaking his head back and forth, he stated, "Good help is so hard to find. Rasheed you're dismissed." Malik fired three rounds, two into his chest and one dead center into his head.

The minute he took to kill Rasheed, Malcom had slipped closer to where he and Shawnee stood. He raised his gun pointing it directly at Shawnee's head. He peered at his brother, although almost identical, Malik barely recognized him. He'd let this way of life in America get the best of him. His stomach bulged outwardly and the dreadlocks he wore were matted.

"This time I am calling the shots." He told Malik.

"Now cooperate and your little bitch here will remain unharmed," he paused to let his words sink in. "It's all up to you Malik."

Malik nodded his head, in understanding. Cautiously observing Malcom who's obsidian eyes told him he was dead serious. Staring at him, he looked worse than the last time he saw him. Outside the sports bar, he pleaded with Malcolm to go home and get his mind right. He had been sucked into a deadly life of cocaine and fast money. He hated seeing his brother this way. It tugged at his heart strings. When Malcom began telling him his latest get rich quick scheme, Malik had heard enough. He turned to leave when Malcolm, struck him from behind. The brawl ended when two bouncers pulled Malik from atop of Malcom and he scurried away promising it wasn't over yet. Now here they stood. Malcolm's voice brought him back to the current state. "Stones. Where are they?" He questioned.

"Malcolm, please." Malik began before being cut off.

"Save the bullshit for someone else, Malik. All I want

are the stones. You can't save me brother dear, but you can save your concubine by giving me the fucking stones now!" Malcom shouted and spittle spewed from his mouth.

"You don't have to do this, Malcolm. I'll give you the stones. Let Shawnee go retrieve them, I left them outside the door." Malik stated.

"Not so fast," Malcolm stated. "You really think I'm stupid enough to let her outta my sight? She stays with me, you go retrieve the stones." Malcom said, grabbing Shawnee forcefully by the arm.

A brief moment passed while Malcolm waited on a reply and Malik stared at Shawnee. Her face was streaked with fresh tears and her eyes were bulbous from crying, but she held her head up high looking defiant and ready to fight. Malik took slow measured steps easing his way upon the two. Standing close enough to see the trembles in Malcolm's hand, Malik lunged at Malcolm sending Shawnee flying to the floor with one hand. He landed a punch right between Malcolm's eyes making his nose bleed.

Dazed from the sudden punch, Malcolm blindly swung the gun towards Malik. Side stepping the impending blow, Malik wrapped one arm around Malcolm's neck. Using all the strength he could muster, Malik squeezed his neck while trying to dislodge the gun in his left hand. Malcolm jerked backward and forward attempting to extricate himself from Malik's hold. Malik increased the pressure until he heard the gun clatter to the floor. Not wanting to waste another second, Malik reached for the gun while attempting to maintain his grip on Malcolm's neck. Malcolm felt the pressure around his neck, loosen and decided it was now or never. With the gun no longer in hand, Malcolm delivered a bone crushing blow into Malik's side causing both the men to fall to the ground.

The ruckus brought Shawnee back to semi-conscious state. Scrambling to get to her feet, Shawnee sprinted towards the warehouse door. Blood streaking down her face from the gash on her forehead, she tripped over the remnants of a broken chair. Crawling over the pieces, she froze in place petrified by the crack of a gunshot yet thankful to hear the shrill of sirens in the distance.

Making her way to the door, Shawnee glanced back and through squinted eyes she saw Malcolm, pushing Malik off the top of him. Shawnee twisted the knob furiously attempting to escape her imprisonment. Flinging the door open, Shawnee ran head first into the hard body of Cruz approaching the other side of the door. The sight of Shawnee's bruised face made him cringe. Before he could examine her any further, Malcolm burst through the warehouse door, yelling, "You made me kill my brother, now you…" Before his last words could be uttered, Cruz removed his glock and fired two shots hitting Malcom in the center of his chest. The loud cracks reverberated off the buildings causing an already terrified Shawnee to shriek. As Malcolm crumbled to the ground, the elm box crashed to the ground as well, expelling stones of various sizes. Astonished, Cruz peered over at Shawnee still crouched down beside the truck. Picking up the jewel beside her feet, Cruz lifted her trembling body as well. Walking around the truck to the passenger side, Cruz gently placed her inside the truck, just as the police he called earlier finally pulled up to the scene.

After talking to the uniformed officers, Cruz boarded the ambulance with the attendants working on Shawnee. As the technician was about to close the door, Cruz heard one of the officers yell in the distance. "We've got a live on inside."

Shawnee pulled the oxygen mask from her face, "How did you find me?" she asked just above a whisper.

"Shhh," Cruz replied. Placing the mask back over her face, he said, "Not now, let the medic take care of you first."

Outside the second ambulance shrieked to a halt. The team of technicians jumped out the back with a gurney in tow racing towards the waving officer. A few minutes later, bloody and barely breathing Malik was strapped to the gurney as the officers followed close behind. The technician returned to work on Shawnee, giving her a mild sedative before reaching back and closing the door.

Cruz stood at Shawnee's side as the doctor finished the delicate task of stitching closed the gash on her forehead. There were bruises as well. Her eye had swollen so badly she could barely see. The physician suggested she stay overnight for observation, but Shawnee refused.

Silent and slightly drowsy from the painkillers the doctor provided, Shawnee left the hospital at Cruz's side. His arms were wrapped protectively around her. His face still etched with fear and concern.

The ride back to his condo, was completely silent. Cruz kept one hand on her knee the entire drive. Too many thoughts were racing through his brain at the moment. All he wanted to do was get her home, he would deal with the rest later.

Arriving back to the condo, Cruz picked up a still sleeping Shawnee, walked her inside, sat her on the bed, and proceeded to remove her blood soaked shirt. He removed her Nikes then wriggled her jeans down her legs. He tossed all the items in a pile that he would send down the incinerator. The garments were too damaged to attempt to save.

Weary, Shawnee awakened as he removed her garments. She watched as he walked from the room, only to return with a couple towels and a basin. He pressed her back a on the bed so her head rested on a down pillow. Gently, he mopped up the remnants of blood that still remained on her face, arms and neck. Shawnee tried to smile, but it turned into more of a scowl with her swollen lip. She focused her eyes on Cruz's face as a lone tear slipped out the side sliding down his weary face. Without saying anything, Shawnee cupped the side of his face slowly wiping the tears away.

"They could've killed you, Shawnee!" Cruz stated, breaking the silence.

143

Shawnee withdrew her hand from his face, her gaze fell on his chest, taking in each rise and fall. She knew what was coming next, yet she didn't have a reasonable explanation of why. Shawnee reached for his hand, removed the towel he was gripping and placed his hand over hers. "Please let's not go there. Right now I don't want to think about how I could've died. I know I could've died. I didn't know that Malcolm was Malik's brother until after the memorial service for Jen. I only went to Malik's place to break it off with him. Then he proposed, but I told him no." Shawnee stated.

"How could you, Shawnee?" Cruz asked. He released her hand, gazing directly into her bruised face. The crinkles in his brow indicated his anger was rising. Reality sunk in and Cruz turned his head. With closed eyes he questioned, "The day I made Jen's memorial arrangements, were you with him? Did you fuck him too?"

"Why would you even think that?" Shawnee responded. "No, I didn't fuck him, since I've been with you. And that is all that matters. Yes I went to see him. But only to tell him about the changes in my life. YOU!"

Struggling to sit up, Shawnee slipped her hands around his neck pulling him closer to her. She whispered, "I love you and only you Derrick Black."

All the rage that was building inside him at the thought of his Shawnee with another man disappeared as her words flooded his eardrum and took the direct route to his heart. He told her numerous times, but this was the first time she uttered it to him. He craved to make love to her right then and have her sing those three little words over and over again. Instead, he wrapped his arms around her and gently kissed her temple. As he lifted her, her one unbruised eye fluttered open. His gaze held so much desire her heart for an instant felt as if it had stopped beating entirely. An ecstasy of emotion flooded through her as he brushed her mouth with a tenuous kiss.

"I love you, Shawnee," he told her again, the passion resonated in his voice and brought tears to her eyes.

Quiet, motionless they lay together. Arms and legs

entangled. She closed her eyes, allowing the painkillers to reclaim her into a semi-comatose state. She needed to forget about her past with Malik and the horrid day she spent captive. Right now all she wanted was holding her tightly in his embrace. As she drifted off, she knew this was the beginning of forever.

Cruz Control

About the Author

*L*aRedeaux began writing as a way to express herself early in life. The Georgia native is an author and CEO at Midnight Publications. LaRedeaux has published several flash fiction and short stories. Coming January 2014 Smiley Face Killers.

Thank you for your purchase!
Other works by LaRedeaux can be
found on www.lovelifewriter.com:

One Man's Desire

'TIL DEATH

SexVentures

OoPs!

FOLLOW ME ON TWITTER!
www.twitter.com/UnRestrictedLuv

Website:

La Redeaux

www.ingramcontent.com/pod-product-compliance
Lightning Source LLC
Chambersburg PA
CBHW070934130626
46555CB00001B/421